SKELETON KEY

Anthony Horowitz says of the Alex Rider books, *Stormbreaker*, *Point Blanc* and *Skeleton Key*; "I had always wanted to write a modern 'teenager saves the world' story. It was a recurring fantasy when I was at school (particularly in geography lessons) that I wasn't a bored thirteen year old stuck in a gruesome north London prep school, but that I was, in reality, an MI6 agent. At the same time, I wanted to make my story seem very credible. So I've researched everything from the rudiments of SAS training to remaining in a car until the very last moment before it's crushed in a breaker's yard, and I get my thirteen-year-old son Nicholas to try out things like diving and snowboarding!"

Anthony is a popular and prolific children's writer, whose books now sell in more than a dozen countries around the world. He has won numerous prizes for his books, which include *Stormbreaker* (shortlisted for the 2000 Children's Book Award) and its sequels *Point Blanc* and *Skeleton Key*; *Groosham Grange* and its sequel *The Unholy Grail*; *Granny* (shortlisted for the 1994 Children's Book Award); and the Diamond Brothers trilogy – *The Falcon's Malteser* (which has been filmed with the title *Just Ask for Diamond*) and two sequels, *South by South East* (which was dramatized in six parts on TV) and *Public Enemy Number Two* – to which three short novels have been added: *I Know What You Did Last Wednesday*, *The French Confection* and *The Blurred Man*. Anthony also writes extensively for TV, with credits including the hit series *Murder in Mind*, as well as *Foyle's War*, *Midsomer Murders*, *Poirot* and *Murder Most Horrid*, and he has been described by the *Radio Times* as "a one man crime-wave". He is married to the television producer Jill Green, and lives in north London with their two children, Nicholas and Cassian, and their dog, Unlucky.

Other Alex Rider books

Stormbreaker
Point Blanc
Eagle Strike

Diamond Brothers books

The Falcon's Malteser
South by South East
Public Enemy Number Two
The Blurred Man
The French Confection
I Know What You Did Last Wednesday

Other books by the same author

The Devil and His Boy
Granny
Groosham Grange
Return to Groosham Grange
The Switch

SKELETON KEY

ANTHONY HOROWITZ

WALKER BOOKS

AND SUBSIDIARIES

LONDON • BOSTON • SYDNEY

To B.B.

First published 2002 by Walker Books Ltd
87 Vauxhall Walk, London SE11 5HJ

This edition published 2003

2 4 6 8 10 9 7 5 3 1

Text © 2002 Anthony Horowitz
Cover illustration © 2002 Phil Schramm
Cover silhouette © 2003 Walker Books Ltd

The right of Anthony Horowitz to be identified as author
of this work has been asserted by him in accordance
with the Copyright, Designs and Patents Act 1988

This book has been typeset in Officina Sans

Printed in Great Britain by J.H. Haynes & Co. Ltd

British Library Cataloguing in Publication Data:
a catalogue record for this book is
available from the British Library

ISBN 0-7445-6587-1

CONTENTS

IN THE DARK

Night came quickly to Skeleton Key.

The sun hovered briefly on the horizon, then dipped below. At once, the clouds rolled in – first red, then mauve, silver, green and black as if all the colours in the world were being sucked into a vast melting pot. A single frigate bird soared over the mangroves, its own colours lost in the chaos behind it. The air was close. Rain hung waiting. There was going to be a storm.

The single engine Cessna Skyhawk SP circled twice before coming in to land. It was the sort of plane that would barely have been noticed, flying in this part of the world. That was why it had been chosen. If anyone had been curious enough to check the registration number printed under the wing, they would have learned that this plane belonged to a photographic company based in Jamaica. This was not true. There was no company and it was already too dark to take photographs.

There were three men in the aircraft. They were all dark skinned, wearing faded jeans and loose, open-neck shirts. The pilot had long black hair, deep brown eyes and a thin scar running down the side of his face. He had met his two passengers only that afternoon. They had introduced themselves as Carlo and Marc but he doubted these were their real names. He knew that their journey had begun a long time ago, somewhere in Eastern Europe. He knew that this short flight was the last leg. He knew what they were carrying. Already, he knew too much.

The pilot glanced down at the multifunction display in the control panel. The illuminated computer screen was warning him of the storm that was closing in. That didn't worry him. Low clouds and rain gave him cover. The authorities were less vigilant during a storm. Even so, he was nervous. He had flown into Cuba many times, but never here. And tonight he would have preferred to have been going almost anywhere else.

Cayo Esqueleto. Skeleton Key.

There it was, stretching out before him, thirty-eight kilometres long and nine kilometres across at its widest point. The sea around it, which had been an extraordinary, brilliant blue until a few minutes ago, had suddenly darkened, as if someone had thrown a switch. Over to the west, he could make out the twinkling lights of Puerto Madre, the island's second biggest town. The main airport was further north, outside the capital of Santiago. But that wasn't where he was heading. He pressed on the joystick and the plane veered to the right, circling over the forests and mangrove swamps that surrounded the old, abandoned airport at the bottom end of the island.

The Cessna had been equipped with a thermal intensifier, similar to the sort used in American spy satellites. He flicked a switch and glanced at the display. A few birds appeared as tiny pinpricks of red. There were more dots pulsating in the swamp. Crocodiles or perhaps manatees. And a single dot about twenty metres from the runway. He turned to speak to the man called Carlo but there was no need. Carlo was already leaning over his shoulder, staring at the screen.

Carlo nodded. There was only one man waiting for them, as agreed. Anyone hiding within a few hundred metres of the airstrip would have shown up. It was safe to land.

The pilot looked out of the window and there was the runway. It was a rough strip of land on the edge of the coast, hacked out of the jungle and running parallel with the sea. The pilot would have missed it altogether in the dying light but for the two lines of electric bulbs burning at ground level, outlining the path for the plane.

The Cessna swooped out of the sky. At the last minute it was buffeted about by a sudden, damp squall that had been sent to try the pilot's nerve. The pilot didn't blink and a moment later the wheels hit the ground and the plane was bouncing and shuddering along, dead centre between the two rows of lights. He was grateful they were there. The mangroves – thick bushes, half-floating on pools of stagnant water – came almost to the edge of the runway. Go even a couple of metres in the wrong direction and a wheel might snag. It would be enough to destroy the plane.

The pilot flicked switches. The engine died and the twin-bladed propellers slowed down and came to a halt. He looked out of the window. There was a jeep parked next to one of the buildings and it was here that the single man – the red dot on his screen – was waiting. He turned to his passengers.

"He's there."

The older of the two men nodded. Carlo was about thirty years old with black, curly hair. He hadn't shaved. Stubble the colour of cigarette ash clung to his jaw. He turned to the other passenger. "Marc? Are you ready?"

The man who called himself Marc could have been Carlo's younger brother. He was barely twenty-five and although he was trying not to show it, he was scared. There was sweat on the side of his face, glowing green as it caught the light from the control panel. He reached behind him and took out a gun, a German-built 10mm Glock automatic. He checked it was loaded, then slipped it into the waistband at the back of his trousers, under his shirt.

"I'm ready," he said.

"There is only him. There are two of us." Carlo tried to reassure Marc. Or perhaps he was trying to reassure himself. "We're both armed. There is nothing he can do."

"Then let's go."

Carlo turned to the pilot. "Have the plane ready," he commanded. "When we walk back, I will give you a sign." He raised a hand, one finger and thumb forming an O. "That is the signal that

11

our business has been successfully concluded. Start the engine at that time. We don't want to stay here one second longer than we have to."

They got out of the plane. There was a thin layer of gravel on the runway which crunched beneath their combat boots as they walked round the side to the cargo door. They could feel the sullen heat in the air, the heaviness of the night sky. The island seemed to be holding its breath. Carlo reached up and opened a door. In the back of the plane was a black container, about one metre by two. With difficulty, he and Marc lowered it to the ground.

The younger man looked up. The lights on the landing strip dazzled him but he could just make out a figure standing still as a statue beside the jeep, waiting for them to approach. He hadn't moved since the plane had landed. "Why doesn't he come to us?" he asked.

Carlo spat and said nothing.

There were two handles, one on either side of the container. The two men carried it between them, walking awkwardly, bending over their load. It took them a long time to reach the jeep. But at last they were there. For a second time, they set the box down.

Carlo straightened up, rubbing his palms on

the side of his jeans. "Good evening, General," he said. He was speaking in English. This was not his native language. Nor was it the general's. But it was the only language they had in common.

"Good evening." The general did not bother with names that he knew would be false anyway. "You had no trouble getting here?"

"No trouble at all, General."

"You have it?"

"One kilogram of weapons grade uranium. Sufficient to build a bomb powerful enough to destroy a city. I would be interested to know which city you have in mind."

General Alexei Sarov took a step forward and the lights from the runway illuminated him. He was not a big man, yet there was something about him that radiated power and control. He still carried with him his years in the army. They could be seen in his close-cut, iron grey hair, his watchful pale blue eyes, his almost emotionless face. They were there in the very way he carried himself. He was perfectly poised; relaxed and wary at the same time. General Sarov was sixty-two years old but looked twenty years younger. He was dressed in a dark suit, a white shirt and a narrow dark blue tie. In the damp heat of the evening, his clothes should have been creased.

He should have been sweating. But to look at him, he could have just stepped out of an air-conditioned room.

He crouched down beside the container, at the same time producing a small device from his pocket. It looked like a car cigarette lighter with a dial attached. He found a socket in the side of the box and plugged the device in. Briefly, he examined the dial. He nodded. It was satisfactory.

"You have the rest of the money?" Carlo asked.

"Of course." The general straightened up and walked over to the jeep. Carlo and Marc tensed themselves – this was the moment when he might produce a gun. But when he turned round he was holding a black leather attaché-case. He flicked the locks and opened it. The case was filled with banknotes: one hundred dollar bills neatly banded together in packets of fifty. One hundred packets in all. A total of half a million dollars. More money than Carlo had ever seen in his life.

But still not enough.

"We've had a problem," Carlo said.

"Yes?" Sarov did not sound surprised.

Marc could feel the sweat as it drew a comma down the side of his neck. A mosquito was whining in his ear but he resisted the urge to slap it. This was what he had been waiting for. He was standing a few steps away, his hands hanging limply by his side. Slowly, he allowed them to creep behind him, closer to the concealed gun. He glanced at the ruined buildings. One might once have been a control tower. The other looked like a customs shed. Both of them were broken and empty, the brickwork crumbling, the windows smashed. Could there be someone hiding there? No. The thermal intensifier would have shown them. They were alone.

"The cost of the uranium." Carlo shrugged. "Our friend in Miami sends his apologies. But there are new security systems all over the world. Smuggling – particularly this sort of thing – has become much more difficult. And that's meant extra expense."

"How much extra expense?"

"A quarter of a million dollars."

"That's unfortunate."

"Unfortunate for you, General. You're the one who has to pay."

Sarov considered. "We had an agreement," he said.

"Our friend in Miami hoped you'd understand."

There was a long silence. Marc's fingers reached

out behind his back, closing around the Glock automatic. But then Sarov nodded. "I will have to raise the money," he said.

"You can have it transferred to the same account that we used before," Carlo said. "But I have to warn you, General. If the money hasn't arrived in three days, the American intelligence services will be told what has happened here tonight ... what you've just received. You may think you are safe here on this island. I can assure you, you won't be safe any more."

"You're threatening me," Sarov muttered. There was something at once calm and deadly in the way he spoke.

"It's nothing personal," Carlo said.

Marc produced a cloth bag. He unfolded it, then tipped the money out of the case and into the bag. The case might contain a radio transmitter. It might contain a small bomb. He left it behind.

"Good night, General," Carlo said.

"Good night." Sarov smiled. "I hope you enjoy the flight."

The two men walked away. Marc could feel the money, the bundles pressing through the cloth against the side of his leg. "The man's a fool," he whispered, returning to his own language.

16

"An old man. Why were we afraid?"

"Let's just get out of here," Carlo said. He was thinking about what the general had said: *I hope you enjoy the flight*. Had he been smiling when he said that?

He made the agreed signal, pressing his finger and thumb together. At once the Cessna's engine started up.

General Sarov was still watching them. He hadn't moved, but now his hand reached once again into his jacket pocket. His fingers closed around the radio transmitter waiting there. He had wondered if it would be necessary to kill the two men and their pilot. Personally, he would have preferred not to, even as an insurance policy. But their demands had made it necessary. He should have known they would be greedy. Given the sort of people they were, it was almost inevitable.

Back in the plane, the two men were strapping themselves into their seats while the pilot prepared for take-off. Carlo heard the engine rev up as the plane slowly began to turn. Far away, there was a low rumble of thunder. Now he wished that they had turned the plane round immediately after they had landed. It would have saved some precious seconds and he was eager to be away, back in the air.

I hope you enjoy the flight.

There had been no emotion whatsoever in the general's voice. He could have meant what he was saying. But Carlo guessed he would have spoken exactly the same way if he had been passing a sentence of death.

Next to him, Marc was already counting the money, running his hands through the piles of notes. He looked back at the ruined buildings, at the waiting jeep. Would Sarov try something? What sort of resources did he have on the island? But as the plane turned in a tight circle, nothing moved. The general stayed where he was. There was nobody else in sight.

The runway lights went out.

"What the...?" The pilot swore viciously.

Marc stopped his counting. Carlo understood at once what was happening. "He's turned the lights off," he said. "He wants to keep us here. Can you take off without them?"

The plane had turned a half-circle so that it was facing the way it had come. The pilot stared out through the cockpit window, straining to see into the night. It was very dark now, but there was an ugly, unnatural light pulsating in the sky. He nodded. "It won't be easy, but..."

The lights came back on again.

There they were, stretching into the distance, an arrow that pointed to freedom and an extra profit of a quarter of a million dollars. The pilot relaxed. "It must have been the storm," he said. "It disrupted the electricity supply."

"Just get us out of here," Carlo muttered. "The sooner we're in the air, the happier I'll be."

The pilot nodded. "Whatever you say." He pressed down on the controls and the Cessna lumbered forward, picking up speed quickly. The runway lights blurred, guiding him forward. Carlo settled back into his seat. Marc was watching out of the window.

And then, seconds before the wheels left the ground, the plane suddenly lurched. The whole world twisted as a giant, invisible hand seized hold of it and wrenched it sideways. The Cessna had been travelling at one hundred and fifty kilometres per hour. It came to a grinding halt in a matter of seconds, the deceleration throwing all three men forward in their seats. If they hadn't been belted in, they would have been hurled out of the front window – or what was left of the shattered glass. At the same time there was a series of ear-shattering crashes as something whipped into the fuselage. One of the wings had dipped down and the propeller was torn off, spinning into the night. Suddenly the plane was still, resting tilted on one side.

For a moment, nobody moved inside the cabin. The plane's engines rattled and stopped. Then Marc pulled himself up in his seat. "What happened?" he screamed. "What happened?" He had bitten his tongue. Blood trickled down his chin. The bag was still open and money had spilled into his lap.

"I don't understand..." The pilot was too dazed to speak.

"You left the runway!" Carlo's face was twisted with shock and anger.

"I didn't!"

"There!" Marc was pointing at something and Carlo followed his quivering finger. The door on the underside of the plane had buckled. Black water was seeping in underneath, forming a pool around their feet.

There was another rumble of thunder, closer this time.

"He did this!" the pilot said.

"What did he do?" Carlo demanded.

"He moved the runway!"

It had been a simple trick. As the plane had turned, Sarov had switched off the lights on the runway using the radio transmitter in his pocket. For a moment, the pilot had been disoriented, lost in the darkness. Then the plane had finished its turn and the lights had come back on. But what he hadn't known, what he wouldn't have been able to see, was that it was a second set of lights that had been activated – and that these ran off at an angle, leaving the safety of the runway and continuing over the surface of the swamp.

"He led us into the mangroves," the pilot said.

Now Carlo understood what had happened to the plane. The moment its wheels touched the water, its fate had been sealed. Without solid ground beneath it, the plane had become bogged down and toppled over. Swamp water was even now pouring in as they slowly sank beneath the surface. The branches of the mangrove trees that had almost torn the plane apart surrounded them, bars of a living prison.

"What are we going to do?" Marc demanded, and suddenly he was sounding like a child. "We're going to drown!"

"We can get out!" Carlo had suffered whiplash injuries in the collision. He moved one arm painfully, unfastening his seat-belt.

"We shouldn't have tried to cheat him!" Marc

cried. "You knew what he was. You were told—"

"Shut up!" Carlo had a gun of his own. He pulled it out of the holster underneath his shirt and balanced it on his knee. "We'll get out of here and we'll deal with him. And then somehow we'll find a way off this damn island."

"There's something..." the pilot began.

Something had moved outside.

"What is it?" Marc whispered.

"Shhh!" Carlo half stood up, his body filling the cramped space of the cabin. The plane tilted again, settling further into the swamp. He lost his balance then steadied himself. He reached out, past the pilot, as if he was going to climb out of the broken front window.

Something huge and horrible lunged towards him, blocking out what little light there was in the night sky. Carlo screamed as it threw itself head first into the plane and onto him. There was a glint of white and a dreadful grunting sound. The other men were screaming too.

General Sarov stood watching. It wasn't raining yet but the water was heavy in the air. There was a flash of lightning that seemed to cross the sky almost in slow motion, relishing its journey. In that moment, he saw the Cessna on its side, half-buried in the swamp. There were now half a dozen crocodiles swarming all over it. The largest of them had dived head first into the cockpit. Only its tail was visible, thrashing about as it gorged itself.

He reached down and lifted up the black container. Although it had taken two men to carry it to him, it seemed to weigh nothing in his hands. He placed it in the jeep, then stood back. He allowed himself the rare privilege of a smile and felt it, briefly, on his lips. Tomorrow, when the crocodiles had finished their meal, he would send in his field workers – the *macheteros* – to recover the banknotes. Not that the money was important. He was the owner of one kilogram of weapons grade uranium. As Carlo had said, he now had the power to destroy a small city.

But Sarov had no intention of destroying a city.

His target was the entire world.

MATCH POINT

Alex caught the ball on the top of his chest, bounced it forward and kicked it into the back of the net. It was then that he noticed the man with the large white dog. It was a warm, bright Friday afternoon, the weather caught between late spring and early summer. This was only a practise match but Alex took the game seriously. Mr Wiseman, who taught PE, had selected him for the first team and he was looking forward to playing against other schools in west London. Unfortunately, his school, Brookland, didn't have its own playing fields. This was a public field and anyone could walk past. And they could bring their dogs.

Alex recognized the man at once and his heart sank. At the same time he was angry. How could he have the nerve to come here, into the school arena, in the middle of a game? Weren't these people ever going to leave him alone?

The man's name was Crawley. With his thinning hair, blotchy face and old-fashioned clothes, he looked like a junior army officer or perhaps a teacher in a second-rate private school. But Alex knew the truth. Crawley belonged to MI6. Not exactly a spy, but someone who was very much a part of that world. Crawley was an office manager in one of the country's most secret offices. He did the paperwork, made the arrangements, set up the meetings. When someone died with a knife in their back or a bullet in their chest, it would be Crawley who had signed on the dotted line.

As Alex ran back to the centre line, Crawley walked over to a bench, dragging the dog behind. The animal didn't seem to want to walk. It didn't want to be there at all. Crawley sat down. He was still sitting there ten minutes later when the final whistle blew and the game came to an end. Alex considered for a moment. Then he picked up his jersey and went over to him.

Crawley seemed surprised to see him. "Alex!" he exclaimed. "What a surprise! I haven't seen you since ... well, since you got back from France."

It had only been four weeks since MI6 had

forced Alex to investigate a school for the super-rich in south-east France. Using a false name, he had become a student at the Point Blanc Academy only to find himself taken prisoner by the mad headmaster, Dr Grief. He had been chased down a mountain, shot at and almost dissected alive in a biology class. Alex had never wanted to be a spy and the whole business had convinced him he was right. Crawley was the last person he wanted to see.

But the MI6 man was beaming. "Are you on the school team? Is this where you play? I'm surprised I haven't noticed you before. Barker and I often walk here."

"Barker?"

"The dog." Crawley reached out and patted it. "He's a Dalmatian."

"I thought Dalmatians had spots."

"Not this one." Crawley hesitated. "Actually, Alex, it's a bit of luck running into you. I wonder if I could have a word with you?"

Alex shook his head. "Forget it, Mr Crawley. I told you the last time. I'm not interested in MI6. I'm a schoolboy. I'm not a spy."

"Absolutely!" Crawley agreed. "This has got nothing to do with the ... um ... company. No, no, no." He looked almost embarrassed. "The thing is, what I wanted to ask you was ... how would you like a front row seat at Wimbledon?"

The question took Alex completely by surprise. "Wimbledon? You mean ... the tennis?"

"That's right." Crawley smiled. "The All England Tennis Club. I'm on the committee."

"And you're offering me a ticket?"

"Yes."

"What's the catch?"

"There is no catch, Alex. Not really. But ... let me explain." Alex was aware that the other players were getting ready to leave. The school day was almost over. He listened as Crawley went on. "The thing is, you see, a week ago we had a break-in. Security at the club is always tight but someone managed to climb over the wall and get into the Millennium Building through a forced window."

"What's the Millennium Building?"

"It's where the players have their changing rooms. It's also got a gym, a restaurant, a couple of lounges and so on. We have closed circuit television cameras but the intruder disabled the system – along with the main alarm. It was a thoroughly professional job. We'd never have known anyone had been there except for a stroke of luck. One of our night guards saw the man leaving. He was Chinese, in his early twenties—"

"The guard?"

"The intruder. Dressed from head to foot in black with some sort of rucksack on his back. The guard alerted the police and we had the whole place searched. The Millennium Building, the courts, the cafés ... everywhere. It took three days. There are no terrorist cells active in London at the moment, thank goodness, but there was always a chance that some lunatic might have planted a bomb. We had the anti-terrorist squad in. Sniffer dogs. Nothing! Whoever it was had vanished into thin air and it seemed he'd left nothing behind.

"Now, here's the strange thing, Alex. He didn't leave anything, but nor did he *take* anything. In fact, nothing seems to have been touched. As I say, if the guard hadn't seen this chap, we'd never have known he had been there. What do you make of that?"

Alex shrugged. "Maybe the guard disturbed him before he could get his hands on whatever it was he wanted."

"No. He was already leaving when he was seen."

"Could the guard have imagined it?"

"We examined the cameras. The film is time-coded and we discovered that they had definitely been out of action for two hours. From midnight until two in the morning."

"Then what do you think, Mr Crawley? Why are you telling me this?"

Crawley sighed and stretched his legs. He was wearing suede shoes, shabby and down at heel. The dog had fallen asleep. "My belief is that somebody is intending to sabotage Wimbledon this year," he said. Alex was about to interrupt but Crawley held up a hand. "I know it sounds ridiculous and I have to admit, the other committee members don't believe me. On the other hand, they don't have my instincts. They don't work in the same business as me. But think about it, Alex. There had to be a reason for such a carefully planned and executed break-in. But there *is* no reason. Something's wrong."

"Why would anyone want to sabotage Wimbledon?"

"I don't know. But you have to remember, the Wimbledon tennis fortnight is a huge business. There are millions of pounds at stake. Prize money alone adds up to eight and a half million. And then there are television rights, merchandising rights, corporate sponsorship... We get VIPs flying in from all over the planet – everyone from film stars to presidents – and tickets for the men's final have been known to change hands for literally thousands of pounds. It's not just a game. It's a world event, and if anything happened ... well, it doesn't bear thinking about."

Crawley obviously had been thinking about it. He looked tired. The worry was deep in his eyes.

Alex thought for a moment. "You want me to look around." He smiled. "I've never been to Wimbledon. I've only ever seen it on TV. I'd love a ticket for Centre Court. But I don't see how a one-day visit would actually help."

"Exactly, Alex. But a one-day visit isn't quite what I had in mind."

"Go on."

"Well, you see, I was wondering if you would consider becoming a ballboy."

"You're not serious?"

"Why not? You can stay there for the whole fortnight. You'll have a wonderful time and you'll be right in the middle of things. You'll see some great matches. And I'll be able to relax a little, knowing you're there. If anything is going on, there's a good chance you might spot it. Then you can call me and I'll take care of it." He nodded. It was obvious that he had managed to persuade himself, if not Alex. "It's not as if this is danger-ous or anything. I mean ... it's Wimbledon. There'll be plenty of other boys and girls there. What d'you think?"

"Don't you have enough security people already?"

"Of course we have a security company. They're easy to see – which makes them easy to avoid. But you'd be invisible, Alex. That's the whole point."

"Alex...?"

It was Mr Wiseman who had called out to him. The teacher was waiting for him. All the other players had left now, apart from two or three boys kicking the ball amongst themselves.

"I'll just be a minute, sir," Alex called back.

The teacher hesitated. It was rather strange, one of the boys talking to this man in his old-fashioned blazer and striped tie. But on the other hand, this was Alex Rider and the whole school knew there was something odd about him. He had been away from school twice recently, both times without any proper explanation, and the last time he had turned up again, the whole science block had been destroyed in a mysterious fire. Mr Wiseman decided to ignore the situation. Alex could look after himself and he would doubtless turn up later. He hoped.

"Don't be too long!" he said.

He walked off and Alex found himself left on his own with Crawley.

He considered what he had just been told. Part of him mistrusted Crawley. Was it just a coincidence, his coming upon Alex on a playing field in the middle of a game? Unlikely. In the world of MI6, where everything was planned and calculated, there were no coincidences. It was one of the reasons why Alex hated it. They had used him twice now, and both times they hadn't really cared if he had lived or died, as long as he was useful to them. Crawley was part of that world and in his heart Alex disliked him as much as the rest of it.

But at the same time, he told himself, he might be reading too much into this. Crawley wasn't asking him to infiltrate a foreign embassy or parachute into Iraq or anything remotely dangerous. He was being offered two weeks at Wimbledon. It was as simple as that. A chance to watch some tennis and – if he was unlucky – spot someone trying to get their hands on the club silver. What could possibly go wrong?

"All right, Mr Crawley," he said. "I don't see why not."

"That's wonderful, Alex. I'll make the arrangements. Come on, Barker!"

Alex glanced at the dog and noticed that it had just woken up. It was staring at him with pink, bloodshot eyes. Warning him? Did the dog know something he didn't?

But then Crawley jerked on the leash and before the dog could give away any of its master's secrets, it was quickly pulled away.

Six weeks later, Alex found himself on Centre Court, dressed in the dark green and mauve colours of the All England Tennis Club. What must surely be the final game in this qualifying round was about to begin. One of the two players sitting just centimetres away from him – would go forward to the next round with a chance of winning the half a million pounds prize money that went with the winner's trophy. The other would be on the next bus home. It was only now, as he knelt beside the net and waited for the serve, that Alex really understood the power of Wimbledon and why it had won its place on the world calendar. There was simply no competition like it.

He was surrounded by the great bulk of the stadium, with thousands and thousands of spectators rising ever higher until they disappeared into the shadows at the very top. It was hard to make out any of the faces. There were too many of them and they seemed too far away. But he felt the thrill of the crowd as the players walked to their ends of the court, the perfectly striped grass seeming to glow beneath their feet. There was a clatter of applause, echoing upwards, and then a sudden stillness. Photographers hung, vulture-like, over huge telephoto lenses while beneath them, in green-covered bunkers, television cameras swung round to take in the first serve. The players faced each other: two men whose whole lives had led up to this moment and whose future in the game would be decided in the next few minutes. It was all so very English – the grass, the strawberries, the straw hats. And yet it was still bloody, a gladiatorial contest like no other.

"Quiet please, ladies and gentlemen…"

The umpire's voice rang out through the various speakers and then the first player served. Jacques Lefevre was French, twenty-two years old and new to the tournament. Nobody had expected him to get this far. He was playing a German, Jamie Blitz, one of the favourites in this year's competition. But it was Blitz who was losing – two sets down, five games to two. Alex watched him as he waited, balancing on the balls of his feet. Lefevre served. The ball thundered close to the centre line. An ace.

"Fifteen love."

Alex was close enough to see defeat in the German's eyes. This was the cruelty of the game; the psychology of it. Lose your mental edge and you could lose everything. That was what had happened to Blitz now. Alex could almost smell it in his sweat. As he walked to the other side of the court to face the next serve, his whole body looked heavy, as if it was taking all his strength just to keep himself there. He lost the next point and the one after. Alex sprinted across the court, snatched up a ball and just had time to roll it up to the ballboy at left base one. Not that it would be needed. It looked as if there would be only one more serve in the game.

And sure enough, Lefevre managed a final ace, falling to his knees, fists clenched in triumph. It was a pose seen hundreds of times before on the courts of Wimbledon and the audience duly rose to its feet, applauding. But it hadn't been a good match. Blitz should have won. Certainly the game shouldn't have ended in three straight sets. He had been terribly off form and the young

Frenchman had walked all over him.

Alex collected the last of the balls and sent them rolling up to the far corner. He stood to attention while the players shook hands, first with each other, then with the umpire. Blitz walked towards him and started packing up his sports bag. Alex studied his face. The German looked dazed, as if he couldn't quite believe he had lost. Then he picked up his things and walked away. He gave one last salute to the audience and walked off the court. Lefevre was still signing autographs for the front row. Blitz had already been forgotten.

"It was a really bad game," Alex said. "I don't know what was wrong with Blitz. He seemed to be sleepwalking half the time."

It was an hour later and Alex was sitting at a table in the Complex, the set of rooms underneath the umpire's office at the corner of Number One Court where the two hundred boys and girls who work throughout the tournament have their meals, get changed and relax. He was having a drink with two other ballboys and a ballgirl. He had become good friends with the girl in the last couple of weeks – so much so that she'd invited him to join her and her family when they went down to Cornwall after Wimbledon finished. She was dark-haired, with bright blue eyes and freckles. She was also a fast runner and very fit. She went to a convent school in Wimbledon and her father was a journalist working in business and current affairs, but there was nothing remotely serious about her. She loved jokes, the ruder the better, and Alex was sure that her laughter could be heard as far away as Court Nineteen. Her name was Sabina Pleasure.

"It's too bad," Sabina said. "But I like Lefevre. He's cute. And he's only a bit older than me."

"Seven years," Alex reminded her.

"That's nothing these days. Anyway, I'll be back on Centre Court tomorrow. It's going to be hard to keep my eye on the game."

Alex smiled. He really liked Sabina, even if she did seem to have a fixation with older men. He was glad now that he had accepted Crawley's offer. "Just make sure you keep your hands on the right balls," he said.

"Rider!" The voice cut through the general chat in the cafeteria and a small, tough-looking man came striding out of a side office. This was Wally Walfor, the ex-RAF sergeant responsible for the ballboys and girls.

"Yes, sir?" Alex had spent four weeks training with Walfor and he had decided that the man was less of a monster than he pretended to be.

"I need someone for standby. Do you mind?"

"No, sir. That's fine." Alex drained his drink and stood up. He was glad that Sabina looked sorry to see him go.

Standby involved waiting outside the umpire's office in case he was needed on one of the courts or anywhere inside the grounds. In fact, Alex would enjoy sitting outside in the sun, watching the crowds. He took his tray back to the counter and was about to leave when he noticed something that made him stop and think.

There was a security guard talking on a public telephone in the corner of the room. There was nothing strange about that. There were always guards posted on the entrance to the Complex and they occasionally slipped down for a glass of water, or perhaps to use the toilet. The guard was talking quickly and excitedly, his eyes shining, as if he was passing on important news. It was impossible to hear what he was saying in the general hubbub of the cafeteria, but even so Alex sidled a little closer in the hope of picking up a few words. And that was when he noticed the tattoo. With so many ballboys and girls in the room and with the cooks busy behind the counter, the temperature had risen. The guard had taken off his jacket. He was wearing a short-sleeved shirt. And there, on his arm, just where the material ended, was a large red circle. Alex had never seen anything quite like it. A plain, undecorated circle with no writing, no sign of a picture. What could it mean?

The guard suddenly turned and saw Alex looking at him. It had happened very quickly and Alex was annoyed with himself for not taking more care. The guard didn't stop talking but he shifted his body so that the arm with the tattoo was away from Alex's view. At the same time, he covered the tattoo with his free hand. Alex smiled at him and gestured, as if he was waiting for the phone. The guard muttered a few more words and hung up. Then he put his jacket back on and moved away. Alex waited until he had gone back upstairs, then followed him. The guard had disappeared. Alex took his place on the bench outside the umpire's office and considered.

A telephone conversation in a crowded cafeteria. It shouldn't have meant anything. But the strange thing was, Alex had seen the guard a short while before, about an hour before the

Blitz/Lefevre game had begun. Alex had been sent over to the Millennium Building to deliver a racquet to one of the other competitors and had been directed to the players' lounge. Climbing the staircase that swept up from the main reception, he had found himself in a large, open area with television monitors on one side and computer terminals on the other, and bright red and blue sofas in between. He knew he was privileged to be there. This was a private place. Venus Williams was sitting on one of the sofas. Tim Henman was watching a game on TV. And there was Jamie Blitz himself, getting a plastic cup of iced mineral water from the dispenser against the far wall.

The guard had also been there. Alex had noticed him standing rather awkwardly near the stairs. He was watching Blitz, but at the same time he was using a mobile phone. At least, that was what it looked like. But Alex had thought at the time that there was something strange about him. Although the mobile was at his ear, he wasn't actually talking. All his attention was on Blitz. Alex had watched as Blitz drank his water and walked away. The guard had walked off a few seconds later.

What had he been doing inside the Millennium

Building? That was the first question Alex asked himself now as he sat in the sunshine, listening to the thwack of distant tennis balls and the applause of an unseen crowd. And there was something else, more puzzling. If the guard had a mobile phone, and if that phone had been working just a few hours ago, why had he needed to make a call from the public telephone in the corner of the Complex? Of course, his battery could have gone down. But even so, why use that particular phone? There were telephones all over the club, up on the surface. Could it be that he didn't want to be seen?

And why did he have a red circle tattooed on his arm? He hadn't wanted that to be seen. Alex was certain he had tried to cover it up.

And there was something else. Maybe it was just coincidence, but the guard, just like the man who had broken into the All England Tennis Club to begin with, was Chinese.

BLOOD AND STRAWBERRIES

Alex didn't make a conscious decision to follow the guard, but over the next few days he seemed drawn to him almost as if by accident. He spotted him twice more; once searching handbags at gate five and again giving directions to a couple of spectators.

Unfortunately, it was impossible to keep track of him all the time. That was the one flaw in Crawley's plan. Alex's job as a ballboy kept him on Centre Court throughout much of the day. The ballboys and girls worked a rotation system, two hours on, two hours off. At best, he could only be a part-time spy. And when he was actually on court, he quickly forgot the guard, the telephone and the entire business of the break-in as he found himself absorbed by the drama of the game.

But two days after Blitz had left Wimbledon, Alex found himself once again shadowing the guard. It was about half an hour before afternoon play was due to begin and Alex was about to report into the Complex when he saw him entering the Millennium Building again. That was strange in itself. The building had its own security staff. The public couldn't get past the reception desk without a pass. So what was he doing inside? Alex glanced at his watch. If he was late, Walfor would yell at him and possibly even move him to one of the less interesting perimeter courts. But there was still time. And he had to admit, his curiosity was aroused.

He went into the Millennium Building. As usual, nobody questioned him. His ballboy uniform was enough. He climbed the stairs, passed through the players' lounge and into the restaurant at the other side. The guard was there, ahead of him. Once again he had his mobile phone in his hand. But he wasn't making a call. He was simply standing, watching the players and the journalists as they finished their lunch.

The dining room was large and modern, with a long buffet for hot food and a central area with salads, cold drinks and fruit. There must have been about a hundred people eating at the tables and Alex recognized one or two famous faces among them. He glanced at the guard. He was standing in a corner, trying not to be noticed. At the same time, his attention seemed to be fixed on a table next to one of the windows. Alex followed the direction of his gaze. There were two men sitting at the table. One was wearing a jacket and tie. The other was in a tracksuit. Alex didn't know the first man but the second was Owen Bryant, another world-class player, an American. He would be playing later that afternoon.

The other man could have been his manager, or perhaps his agent. The two of them were talking, quietly, intensely. The manager spoke and Bryant laughed. Alex moved further into the restaurant, keeping close to the wall. He wanted to see what the guard was going to do, but he didn't want to be seen. He was glad that the restaurant was fairly crowded. There were enough people moving about to screen him.

Bryant stood up. Alex saw the guard's eyes narrow. Now the mobile phone was on its way to his ear. But he hadn't dialled a number. Bryant went over to a water dispenser and pulled a cup out of the plastic cylinder. The guard pressed a button on his phone. Bryant helped himself to some water. Alex watched as a bubble of air mushroomed up to the surface inside the plastic tank. The tennis player carried the water back to the table and sat down. The manager said something. Bryant drank his water. And that was it. Alex had seen the whole thing.

But what *had* he seen?

He had no time to answer the question. The guard was already moving, heading for the exit. Alex came to a decision. The main door was between himself and the guard and now he made for it too, keeping his head low as if he wasn't looking where he was going. He timed it perfectly. Just as the guard reached the door, Alex crashed into him. At the same moment, he swung an arm carelessly, knocking the guard's hand. The mobile phone fell to the floor.

"Oh – I'm sorry," Alex said. Before the guard could stop him, he had leant down and picked up the phone. He weighed it in his hand for a moment before passing it back. "Here you are," he said.

The guard said nothing. For a moment his eyes were locked into Alex's and Alex found himself being inspected by two very black pupils that had no life at all. The man's skin was pale and pockmarked, with a sheen of sweat across his upper lip. There was no expression anywhere on his face. Alex felt the telephone being wrenched out of his hand and then the guard had gone, the door swinging shut behind him.

Alex's hand was still in mid-air. He looked down at his palm. He was worried that he had given himself away, but at least he had learned something from the exchange. The mobile phone was a fake. It was too light. There was nothing on the screen. And it had no recognizable logo: Nokia, Panasonic, Virgin ... nothing.

He turned back to the two men at the table. Bryant had finished his water and crumpled the plastic cup in his hand. He was shaking hands with his friend, about to leave.

The water...

Alex had had an idea that was completely absurd and yet made some sort of sense out of what he had seen. He walked back across the restaurant and crouched down beside the dispenser. He had seen the same machines all over the tennis club. He took a cup and used its rim to press the tap underneath the tank. Water, filtered and chilled, ran into the cup. He could feel it, ice cold against his palm.

"What the hell do you think you're doing?"

Alex looked up to see a red-faced man in a Wimbledon blazer towering over him. It was the first unfriendly face he'd seen since he had arrived. "I was just getting some water," he explained.

"I can see that! That's obvious. I mean, what are you doing in this restaurant? This is reserved for players, officials and press."

"I know that," Alex said. He forced himself not to lose his temper. He had no right to be here and if the official – whoever he was – complained, he might well lose his place as a ballboy. "I'm sorry, sir," he said. "I brought a racquet over for Mr Bryant. I delivered it just now. But I was thirsty, so I stopped to get a drink."

The official softened. Alex's story sounded perfectly reasonable. And he had enjoyed being addressed as "sir". He nodded. "All right. But I don't want to see you in here again." He reached out a hand and took the plastic cup. "Now on your way."

Alex arrived back at the Complex about ten minutes before play began. Walfor glowered at him but said nothing.

That afternoon, Owen Bryant lost his match against Jacques Lefevre, the same unknown Frenchman who had so unexpectedly beaten Jamie Blitz two days before. The final score was 6–4, 6–7, 4–6, 2–6. Although Bryant had won the first game, his play had steadily deteriorated throughout the afternoon. It was another surprising result. Like Blitz, Bryant had been a favourite to win.

Twenty minutes later, Alex was back in the basement restaurant, sitting with Sabina, who was drinking a Coke Lite.

"My mum and dad are here today," she was saying. "I managed to get them tickets and in return they've promised to get me a new surfboard. Have you ever surfed, Alex?"

"What?" Alex was miles away.

"I was talking about Cornwall. Surfing..."

"Yes, I've surfed." Alex had learned with his uncle, Ian Rider. The spy whose death had so abruptly changed Alex's life. The two of them had spent a week together in San Diego, California. That had been years ago. Years that sometimes felt like centuries.

"Is there something wrong with your drink?" Sabina asked.

Alex realized he was holding his Coke in front of him, balancing it in his hand, staring at it. But he was thinking about water.

"No, it's fine..." he began.

And then, out of the corner of his eye, he saw

the guard. He had come back downstairs into the Complex. Once again he was using the telephone in the corner. Alex saw him put in a coin and dial a number.

"I'll be right back," he said.

He got up and made his way over to the phone. The guard was standing with his back to him. This time he might be able to get close enough to hear what was being said.

"...will be completely successful." The guard was talking in English but with a thick accent. He still had his back to Alex. There was a pause. Then: "I'm going to meet him now. Yes ... straight away. He'll give it to me and I'll bring it to you." Another pause. Alex got the feeling that the conversation was coming to an end. He took a few steps back. "I have to go," the guard said. "Bye." He put the receiver down and walked away.

"Alex...?" Sabina called to him. She was on her own, sitting where he had left her. He realized she must have been watching what he did. He raised a hand and waved to her. He would have to find some way to explain all this later.

The guard didn't climb back up to the surface. Instead he took a door which led to a long corridor, stretching into the distance. Alex opened the door and followed.

The All England Tennis Club covers a huge area. On the surface it looks a bit like a theme park, though one whose only theme is tennis. Thousands of people stream along paths and covered walkways, an uninterrupted flow of brilliant white shirts, sunglasses and straw hats. As well as the courts, there are tearooms and cafés, restaurants, shops, hospitality tents, ticket booths and security points.

But there is a second, less well-known world underneath all this. The entire club is connected by an underground maze of corridors, tunnels and roads, some big enough to drive a car through. If it's easy to get lost above ground, it's even easier to lose yourself below. There are very few signs and there's nobody standing at the corner to offer you information. This is the world of the cooks and the waiters, the refuse collectors and the delivery men. Somehow they find their way around, coming up in the daylight exactly where they are needed before disappearing again.

The corridor in which Alex found himself was called the Royal Route and connected the Millennium Building with Court Number One, allowing the players to make their way to the game without being seen. It was clean and empty, with a bright blue carpet. The guard was about twenty metres ahead of him and it felt eerie to be so suddenly alone. There were just the two of them there. Above them, on the surface, there would be people everywhere, milling about in the sunlight. Alex was grateful for the carpet, which muffled the sound of his feet. It seemed that the guard was in a hurry. So far he hadn't stopped or turned round.

The guard reached a wooden door marked RESTRICTED. Without stopping, he went through. Alex paused for a moment, then followed. Now he found himself in an altogether grimier environment, a cement corridor with yellow industrial markings and fat ventilation pipes overhead. The air smelled of oil and garbage, and Alex knew that he had arrived at the so-called Buggy Route, a supply lane that forms a great circle underneath the club. A couple of teenagers in green aprons and jeans walked past him, pushing two plastic bins. A waitress went the other way, carrying a tray of dirty plates. There was no sign of the guard and for a moment Alex thought he'd lost him. But then he saw a figure disappearing behind a series of translucent plastic strips that hung from the ceiling to the floor. He could just make out the man's uniform on the other side of the barrier. He hurried forward and went through.

Alex realized two things at the same moment. He no longer had any idea where he was – and he was there on his own.

He was in an underground chamber, banana-shaped, curving round, with concrete pillars supporting the roof. It looked like an underground carpark and there were indeed three or four cars parked in bays next to the raised walkway where he was standing now. But most of the space was taken up by trash. There were empty cardboard boxes, wooden pallets, a rusting cement mixer, bits of old fencing and broken down coffee vending machines, thrown out and left to rot on the damp cement floor. The air smelled bad and Alex could hear a constant whine, like an electric saw, coming from a garbage compactor just out of his sight. And yet the area was also used for the storage of food and drink. There were beer barrels, hundreds of bottles of fizzy drinks, gas cylinders and, clustered together, eight or nine massive white boxes – refrigerators, each one carrying the label RAWLINGS REFRIGERATION.

Alex looked up at the roof. It was slanting upwards and the shape reminded him of something. Of course! The raked seating around Court

Number One! That was where he was – in the loading bay beneath the tennis court. This was the underbelly of Wimbledon all right. This was where all the supplies arrived and where all the trash left. And right now, ten thousand people were sitting just a few metres above his head, enjoying the game, unaware that everything they consumed throughout the day began and ended here.

But where was the guard? Why had he come here and who was he going to meet? Alex crept forward carefully, once again feeling very alone. He was on a raised platform with the single word DANGER repeated in yellow letters along its edge. He didn't need to be told. He came to a flight of steps and went down, moving into the main body of the chamber, on the same level as the refrigerators. He walked past a stack of gas cylinders, pressurized carbon dioxide. He had no idea what they were for. Half the things down here seemed to have been dumped for no good reason.

He was fairly sure now that the guard had gone. Why would he want to meet anyone down here? For the first time since he had left the Complex, Alex played back the telephone conversation in his mind.

I'm going to meet him now. Yes ... straight away. He'll give it to me...

It sounded ridiculous, fake, like something out of a bad film. Even as Alex realized this and knew that he had been tricked, he heard the screaming sound, saw the dark shape rushing out of the shadows. He was in the middle of the concrete floor, out in the open. The guard was behind the wheel of a fork-lift truck, the metal prongs jutting out towards him like the horns of an enormous bull. Powered by its forty-eight volt electric engine, the truck was speeding towards him on pneumatic tyres. Alex glanced up and saw the heavy wooden pallets, a dozen of them, balanced high above the cabin. He saw the guard's smile, a gleam of ugly teeth in an uglier face. The truck covered the distance between them with astonishing speed then came to a sudden halt as the guard slammed on the brake. Alex yelled and threw himself to one side. The wooden pallets, carried forward by the truck's momentum, slid off the forks and came clattering down. Alex should have been crushed, would have been, but for the beer barrels. A line of them had taken the weight of the pallets, leaving a tiny triangle of space. Alex heard the wood smashing centimetres above his head. Splinters rained down on his neck and back. Dust and dirt smothered him. But he was still alive. Choking and half blinded, he crawled forward as the fork-lift truck reversed and prepared to come after him again.

How could he have been so stupid? The guard had seen him that first time in the Complex, when he had made his telephone call. Alex had stood there, gaping at the tattoo on the man's arm and had thought that his ballboy uniform would be enough to protect him. And then, in the Millennium Building, Alex had clumsily knocked into him to get his hands on the mobile phone. Of course the guard had known who he was and what he was doing. It didn't matter that he was a teenager. He was dangerous. He had to be taken out.

And so he had laid a trap so obvious that it wouldn't have fooled ... well, a schoolboy. Alex might want to think of himself as some sort of superspy who had twice saved the whole world, but that was nonsense. The guard had made a fake phone call and tricked Alex into following him into this desolate area. And now he was going to kill him. It wouldn't matter who he was or how much he had found out once he was dead.

Choking and sick, Alex staggered to his feet just as the fork-lift truck bore down on him a second time. He turned and ran. The guard looked almost ridiculous, hunched up in the tiny cabin. But the machine he was driving was fast, powerful and incredibly flexible, spinning a full circle on a ten pence piece. Alex tried changing direction, sprinting to one side. The truck spun round and followed. Could he make it back to the raised platform? No. Alex knew it was too far away.

Now the guard reached out and pressed a button. The metal forks shuddered and dropped down so that they were less like horns, more like the twin swords of some nightmare medieval knight. Which way should he dive? Left or right? Alex just had time to make up his mind before the truck was on him. He dived to the right, rolling over and over on the concrete. The guard pulled the joystick and the machine spun round again. Alex twisted and the heavy wheels missed him by barely a centimetre, then crashed into one of the pillars.

There was a pause. Alex got up, his head spinning. For a brief second, he hoped that the collision might have knocked the guard out, but with a sick feeling in his stomach he saw the man step out of the cabin, brushing a little dust off the arm of his jacket. He was moving with the slow confidence of a man who knew that he was in total command. And Alex could already see why. Automatically, the guard had taken the stance of a martial arts expert; feet slightly apart, centre of gravity low. His hands were curving in the air, waiting to strike. He was still smiling. All he could see was a defenceless boy – and one already weakened by two encounters with the fork-lift truck.

With a sudden cry, he lashed out, his right hand slicing towards Alex's throat. If the blow had made contact, Alex would have been killed. But at the last second he brought up both his fists, crossing his arms to form a block. The guard was taken by surprise and Alex took advantage of the moment to kick out with his right foot, aiming for the groin. But the guard was no longer there, having swivelled to one side, and in that moment Alex knew he was up against a fighter who was stronger, faster and more experienced than him and that he really didn't have a chance.

The guard swung round, and this time the back of his hand caught Alex on the side of his head. Alex heard the crack. For a moment he was blinded. He reeled backwards, crashing into a metal surface. It was the door of one of the fridges. Somehow he caught hold of the handle and as he stumbled forward, the door opened. He felt a blast of cold across the back of his neck and perhaps that was what revived him and gave him the strength to throw himself forward, ducking underneath another vicious kick that had been aimed at his throat.

Alex was in a bad way and he knew it. His nose was bleeding. He could feel the warm blood trickling down over the corner of his mouth. His head was spinning and the electric light bulbs seemed to be flashing in front of his eyes. But the guard wasn't even breathing heavily. For the first time, Alex wondered what it was that he had stumbled onto. What could be so important to the guard that he would be ready to murder a fourteen-year-old boy in cold blood, without even asking questions? Alex wiped the blood away from his mouth and cursed Crawley for coming to him on the football pitch, cursed himself for listening. A front row seat at Wimbledon? At Wimbledon cemetery, perhaps.

The guard started walking towards him. Alex tensed himself, then dived out of the way, avoiding a lethal double strike of foot and fist. He landed next to a dustbin, overflowing with rubbish. Using all his strength, he picked it up and threw it, grinning through gritted teeth as the bin crashed into his attacker, spilling rotting food all over him. The guard swore and stumbled backwards. Alex ran round the back of the fridge, trying to catch his breath, searching for a way out.

He had only seconds to spare. He knew that the guard would be coming after him and next time he would finish it. He'd had enough. Alex looked left and right. He saw the cylinders of compressed gas and dragged one out of its wire frame. The cylinder seemed to weigh a ton but Alex was desperate. He wrenched the tap on and heard the gas jetting out. Then, holding the cylinder in front of him with both hands, he stepped forward. At that moment, the guard appeared round the side of the fridge. Alex jerked forward, his muscles screaming, shoving the cylinder into the man's face. The gas exploded into the man's eyes, temporarily blinding him. Alex brought the cylinder down, then up again. The metal rim clanged into the guard's head, just above his nose. Alex felt the jolt of solid steel against bone. The guard reeled back. Alex took another step forward. This time he swung the cylinder like a cricket bat, hitting the man with incredible force in the shoulders and neck. The guard never had a chance. He didn't even cry out as he was thrown off his feet and sent hurtling forward into the open fridge.

Alex dropped the cylinder and groaned. It felt as if his arms had been wrenched out of their sockets. His head was still spinning and he wondered if his nose had been broken. He limped forward and looked into the fridge.

There was a curtain of plastic sheets and behind it a mountain of cardboard boxes, each and every one of them filled to the brim with strawberries. Alex couldn't help smiling. Strawberries and cream was one of Wimbledon's greatest traditions, served at crazy prices in the kiosks and restaurants above ground. This was where they were stored. The guard had landed in the middle of the boxes, crushing many of them. He was unconscious, half buried in a blanket of strawberries, his head resting on a bright red pillow of them. Alex stood in the doorway, leaning on the frame for support, allowing the cold air to wash over him. There was a thermostat next to him. Outside, the weather was hot. The strawberries had to be kept chilled.

He took one last look at the man who had tried to kill him.

"Out cold," he said.

Then he reached out and twisted the thermostat control, sending the temperature down below zero.

Out colder.

He closed the fridge door and limped painfully away.

THE CRIBBER

It had taken the engineer just a few minutes to take the water dispenser apart. Now he reached inside and carefully disengaged a slim glass phial from a tangle of wires and circuit boards.

"Built into the filter," he said. "There's a valve system. Very ingenious."

He passed the phial to a stern-looking woman who held it up to the light, examining its contents. The phial was half filled with a transparent liquid. She swilled it round, applied a little to her index finger and sniffed it. Her eyes narrowed. "Librium," she announced. She had a clipped, matter-of-fact way of speaking. "Nasty little drug. A spoonful will put you out cold. A couple of drops, though ... they'll just confuse you. Basically knock you off balance."

The restaurant, and indeed the entire Millennium Building, had been closed for the night. There were three other men there. John Crawley was one. Next to him stood a uniformed policeman, obviously senior. The third man was white-haired and serious, wearing a Wimbledon tie. Alex was sitting to one side, feeling suddenly tired and out of place. Nobody apart from Crawley knew that he worked for MI6. As far as they were concerned, he was just a ballboy who had somehow stumbled on the truth.

Alex was dressed in his own clothes now. He had phoned Crawley, then taken a shower and changed, leaving his ballboy uniform back in his locker. Somehow he knew that he had worn it for the last time. He wondered if he would be allowed to keep the shorts, shirt and Hi-Tec trainers with the crossed racquets logo embroidered on the tongue. The uniform is the only payment Wimbledon ballboys and girls receive.

"It's pretty clear what was going on," Crawley was saying now. "You remember, I was worried about that break-in we had, Sir Norman." This to the man in the club tie. "Well, it seems I was right. They didn't want to steal anything. They came here to fix up the water dispensers. In the restaurant, in the lounge and probably all over the building. Remote control ... is that right, Henderson?"

Henderson was the man who had taken the water dispenser apart. Another MI6 operative. "That's right, sir," he replied. "The dispenser functioned perfectly normally, giving out iced water. But when it received a radio signal – and that's what our friend was doing with the fake mobile phone – it injected a few millilitres of this drug, Librium. Not enough to show up in a random blood test if anybody happened to be tested. But enough to destroy their game."

Alex remembered the German player, Blitz, leaving the court after he'd lost his match. He had looked dazed and out of focus. But he had been more than that. He had been drugged.

"It's transparent," the woman added. "And it has virtually no taste. In a cup of iced water it wouldn't have been noticed."

"But I don't understand!" Sir Norman cut in. "What was the point?"

"I think I can answer that," the policeman said. "As you know, the guard isn't talking, but the tattoo on his arm would indicate that he is – or was – a member of the Big Circle."

"And what exactly would that be?" Sir Norman spluttered.

"It's a triad, sir. A Chinese gang. The triads, of course, are involved in a range of criminal activities. Drugs. Vice. Illegal immigration. And gambling. I would guess this operation was related to the latter. Like any other sporting event, Wimbledon attracts millions of pounds' worth of bets. Now, as I understand it, the young Frenchman – Lefevre – began the tournament with odds of three hundred to one against his actually winning."

"But then he beat Blitz and Bryant," Crawley said.

"Exactly. I'm sure Lefevre had no idea, person-ally, what was going on. But if all his opponents were drugged before they went onto the court... Well, it happened twice. It could have gone on right up to the final. Big Circle would have made a killing! A hundred thousand pounds bet on the Frenchman would have brought them thirty million."

Sir Norman stood up. "The important thing now is that nobody finds out about this," he said. "It would be a national scandal and disastrous for our reputation. In fact we'd probably have to begin the whole tournament again!" He glanced at Alex but spoke to Crawley. "Can this boy be trusted not to talk?" he asked.

"I won't tell anyone what happened," Alex said.

"Good. Good."

The policeman nodded. "You did a very good job," he added. "Spotting this chap in the first place and then following him and all the rest of it. Although, I have to say, I think it was rather irresponsible to lock him in the deep freeze."

"He tried to kill me," Alex said.

"Even so! He could have frozen to death. As it is, he may well have lost a couple of fingers from frostbite."

"I hope that won't spoil his tennis playing."

"Well, I don't know..." The policeman coughed. He was clearly unable to make Alex out. "Anyway, well done. But next time, do try to think what you're doing. I'm sure you wouldn't want anyone to get hurt!"

To hell with the lot of them!

Alex stood watching the waves, black and silver in the moonlight as they rolled into the sweeping curve of Fistral Beach. He was trying to put the policeman, Sir Norman and the whole of Wimbledon out of his mind. He had more or less saved the entire All England Tennis Tournament and although he hadn't been expecting a season ticket in the royal box and tea with the Duchess of Kent, nor had he thought he would be bundled out quite so hastily. He had watched the finals, on his own, on TV. At least they'd let him keep his ballboy uniform.

And there was one other good thing that had come out of it all. Sabina hadn't forgotten her invitation.

He was standing on the veranda of the house her parents had rented, a house that would have been ugly anywhere else in the world but which seemed perfectly suited to its position on the edge of a cliff overlooking the Cornish coast. It was old-fashioned, square, part brick, part white-painted wood. It had five bedrooms, three staircases and too many doors. Its garden was more dead than alive, blasted by salt and sea spray. The house was called Brook's Leap, although nobody knew who Brook was, why he had leapt, or even if he had survived. Alex had been there for three days. He had been invited to stay the week.

There was a movement behind him. A door had opened and Sabina Pleasure stepped out, wrapped in a thick towelling robe, carrying two glasses. It was warm outside. Although it had been raining when Alex arrived – it nearly always seemed to be raining in Cornwall – the weather had cleared and this was suddenly a summer's night. Sabina had left him outside while she went in to have a bath. Her hair was still wet. The robe fell loosely down to her bare feet. Alex thought she looked much older than her fifteen years.

"I brought you a Coke," she said.

"Thanks."

The veranda was wide, with a low balcony, a swing chair and a table. Sabina set the glasses down then sat down herself. Alex joined her. The wooden frame of the swing chair creaked and they swung together, looking out at the view. For a long time neither of them said anything. Then, suddenly...

"Why don't you tell me the truth?" Sabina asked.

"What d'you mean?"

"I was just thinking about Wimbledon. Why did you leave straight after the quarter finals? You were there one minute. Court Number One! And then—"

"I told you," Alex cut in, feeling uncomfortable. "I wasn't well."

"That's not what I heard. There was a rumour that you were involved in some sort of fight. And that's another thing. I've noticed you in your swimming shorts. I've never seen anyone with so many cuts and bruises."

"I'm bullied at school."

"I don't think so. I've got a friend who goes to Brookland. She says you're never there. You keep disappearing. You were away twice last term and the day you got back, half the school burned down."

Alex leaned forward and picked up his Coke, rolling the cold glass between his hands. An aeroplane was crossing the sky, tiny in the great darkness, its lights blinking on and off.

"All right, Sab," he said. "I'm not really a schoolboy. I'm a spy, a teenage James Bond. I have to take time off from school to save the world. I've done it twice so far. The first time was here in Cornwall. The second time was in France. What else do you want to know?"

Sabina smiled. "All right, Alex. Ask a stupid question..." She drew her legs up, snuggling into the warmth of the towelling robe. "But there *is* something different about you. You're like no boy I've ever met."

"Kids?" Sabina's mother was calling out from the kitchen. "Shouldn't you be thinking about bed?"

It was ten o'clock. The two of them would be getting up at five to catch the surf.

"Five minutes!" Sabina called back.

"I'm counting."

Sabina sighed. "Mothers!"

But Alex had never known his mother.

Twenty minutes later, getting into bed, he thought about Sabina Pleasure and her parents; her father a slightly bookish man with long grey hair and spectacles, her mother round and cheerful, more like Sabina herself. There were only the three of them. Maybe that was what made them so close. They lived in west London and rented this house for four weeks every summer.

He turned off the light and lay back in the darkness. His room, set high up in the roof of the house, had only one small window and he could see the moon, glowing white, as perfectly round as a one penny piece. From the moment he had arrived, they'd treated him as if they'd known him all his life. Every family has its own routine and Alex had been surprised how quickly he had fallen in with theirs, joining them on long walks along the cliffs, helping with the shopping and the cooking, or simply sharing the silence – reading and watching the sea.

Why couldn't he have had a family like this? Alex felt an old, familiar sadness creep up on him.

69

His parents had died before he was even a few weeks old. The uncle who had brought him up and who had taught him so much had still been, in many ways, a stranger to him. He had no brothers or sisters. Sometimes he felt as isolated as the plane he had seen from the veranda, making its long journey across the night sky, unnoticed and alone.

Alex pulled the pillows up around his head, annoyed with himself. He had friends. He enjoyed his life. He'd managed to catch up with his work at school and he was having a great holiday. And with a bit of luck, with the Wimbledon business behind him, MI6 would leave him alone. So why was he letting himself slip into this mood?

The door opened. Somebody had come into his room. It was Sabina. She was leaning over him. He felt her hair fall against his cheek and smelled her faint perfume; flowers and white musk. Her lips brushed gently against his.

"You're much cuter than James Bond," she said.

And then she was gone. The door closed behind her.

Five-fifteen the next morning.

If this had been a schoolday, Alex wouldn't have woken up for another two hours, and even then he would have dragged himself out of bed unwillingly. But this morning he had been awake in an instant. He had felt the energy and tension coursing through him. And walking down to Fistral Beach with the dawn light pink in the sky, he could feel it still. The sea was calling to him, daring him to come in.

"Look at the waves!" Sabina said.

"They're big," Alex muttered.

"They're huge. This is amazing!"

It was true. Alex had been surfing twice before – once in Norfolk, once with his uncle in California – but he had never seen anything like this. There was no wind. The local radio station had warned of deep water squalls and an exceptionally high tide. Together these had produced waves that took his breath away. They were at least ten feet high, rolling slowly inland as if they carried the weight of the whole ocean on their shoulders. The crash as they broke was huge, terrifying. Alex could feel his heart pounding. He looked at the moving walls of water, the dark blue, the foaming white. Was he really going to ride one of these monsters on a flimsy board made of nothing more than a strip of fibreglass?

Sabina had seen him hesitate. "What d'you think?" she asked.

"I don't know..." Alex replied and realized he was shouting to make himself heard above the roar of the waves.

"The sea's too strong!" Sabina was a good surfer. The morning before, Alex had watched her skilfully manoeuvring some nasty reefbreaks close to the shore. But now she looked uncertain. "Maybe we should go back to bed!" she yelled.

Alex took in the whole scene. There were another half-dozen surfers on the beach and, in the far distance, a man steadying a jet ski in the shallow water. He knew that he and Sabina would be the youngest people there. Like her, he was wearing a three millimetre neoprene wetsuit and boots which would protect him from the cold. So why was he shivering? Alex didn't have his own board but had rented an Ocean Magic thruster. Sabina's was a wider, thicker board, going for stability rather than speed, but Alex preferred the thruster for its grip and the feeling of control provided by its three fins. He was glad also that he had chosen an eight-foot-four. If he was going to catch waves as big as these, he was going to need the extra length.

If...

Alex wasn't sure he was going into the water. The waves looked about twice as tall as him and he knew that if he made a mistake he could all too easily get killed. Sabina's parents had forbidden her to go in if the sea looked too rough and he had to admit, it had never looked rougher. He watched another wave come crashing down and might have turned back if he hadn't heard one surfer calling to another, the words whipping across the empty sands.

"The Cribber!"

It couldn't be true. The Cribber had come to Fistral Beach. Alex had heard the name many times. The Cribber had become a legend not just in Cornwall but throughout the surfing world. Its first recorded visit had been in September 1966, more than twenty feet high, the most powerful wave ever to hit the English coast. Since then there had been occasional sightings, but few had seen it and fewer still had managed to take the ride.

"The Cribber! The Cribber!" The other surfers were calling its name, whooping and shouting. He watched them dance across the sand, their boards over their heads. Suddenly he knew that he had to go into the water. He was too young. The waves were too big. But he would never forgive himself if he missed the chance.

"I'm going!" he shouted and ran forward, carrying his board in front of him, the tail connected to his ankle by a tough urethane leash. Out of the corner of his eye he saw Sabina raise a hand in a gesture of good luck, but by then he had reached the edge of the sea and felt the cold water grip his ankles. He threw the board down and dived on top of it, the momentum carrying him forward. And then he was lying flat on his stomach, his legs stretched out behind him, his hands paddling furiously over the top of the board. This was the most exhausting part of the journey. Alex concentrated on his arms and shoulders, keeping the rest of his body still. He had a long way to go. He needed to conserve energy.

He heard a sound above the pounding of the sea and noticed the jet ski pulling away from the shore. That puzzled him. PWCs – personal water craft – were rare in Cornwall and he certainly hadn't seen this one before. Normally they were used to tow surfers out to the bigger waves, but this jet ski was striking out on its own. He could see the rider, hooded, in a black wetsuit. Was he – or she – planning to ride the Cribber on a machine?

He forgot about it. His arms were getting tired now and he hadn't even made it halfway. His cupped hands scooped the water and he felt himself shoot forward. The other surfers were well ahead of him. He could see the point where the waves crested, about twenty metres away. A mountain of water rose up in front of him and he duck-dived through it. For a moment he was blind. He tasted salt and the chill of the water hammered into his skull. But then he was out the other side. He fixed his eyes on the horizon and redoubled his efforts. The thruster carried him forward as if it had somehow been filled with a life of its own.

Alex stopped and drew breath. Suddenly everything seemed very silent. He was still lying on his stomach, rising and falling as he was swept over the waves. He looked back at the shoreline and was surprised to see how far he had come. Sabina was sitting watching him, a tiny speck in the distance. The nearest surfer was about thirty metres away; too far to help if anything went wrong. There was a knot of fear in his stomach and he wondered if he hadn't been a bit hasty, coming out here on his own. But it was too late now.

He sensed it before he saw it. It was as if the world had chosen that moment to come to an end and all nature was taking one final breath. He turned and there it was. The Cribber was coming. It was hurtling towards him. Now it was too late to change his mind.

For a few seconds Alex stared in astonishment at the rolling, curving, thundering water. It was like watching a four-storey building wrench itself out of the ground and hurl itself onto the street. It was built entirely out of water, but the water was alive. Alex could feel its incredible strength. Suddenly, awesomely, it rose up in front of him. And went on rising until it had blotted out the sky.

Techniques that he had learned a long time ago took over automatically. Alex grabbed the edge of the board and turned round so that he was once again facing the shore. He forced himself to wait until the last second. Move too late and he would miss everything. But too early and he would simply be crushed. His muscles tensed. His teeth were chattering. His whole body seemed to have become electrified.

Now!

This was the most difficult part, the movement that was hardest to learn but impossible to forget. The pop-up. Alex could feel the board travelling with the pulse of the wave. His speed and the speed of the water had become one. He brought his hands down, flat on the board, arched his back and pushed. At the same time, he brought his right leg forward. Goofy-footed. When he was snowboarding, he was exactly the same. But he didn't care, as long as he could actually stand up without losing his balance, and already he was doing just that, balancing the two main forces, speed and gravity, as the thruster sliced diagonally across the wave.

He stood straight, his arms out, his teeth bared, perfectly centred on the board. He had done it! He was riding the Cribber. Sheer exhilaration coursed through him. He could feel the power of the wave. He was part of it. He was plugged into the world and although he must be travelling at sixty, seventy kilometres per hour, time seemed to have slowed down almost to a halt and he was frozen in this one, perfect moment that would be with him for the rest of his life. He yelled out loud, an animal cry that he couldn't even hear. Spray rushed into his face, exploding around him. He could barely feel the thruster under his feet. He was flying. He had never been more alive.

And then he heard it over the roar of the waves. It was coming up fast to one side of him, the whine of a petrol engine. To hear anything mechanical here, at this time, was so unlikely that he thought he must have imagined it. Then he remembered the jet ski. It must have gone out to sea and then circled round, behind the waves. Now it was coming in fast.

His first thought was that the rider was

"dropping in". It was one of the unwritten laws of surfing. Alex was up and riding. This was his wave. The rider had no right to cut into his space. But at the same time, he knew that was crazy. Fistral Beach was practically deserted. There was no need to fight for space. And anyway, a jet ski coming after a surfer ... it was unheard of.

The engine was louder now. Alex couldn't see the jet ski. His entire concentration was fixed on the Cribber, on keeping his balance, and he didn't dare turn round. He was suddenly aware of the rushing water, thousands of gallons of it, thundering under his feet. If he fell he would die, ripped apart before he could drown. What was the jet ski doing? Why was it coming so close?

Alex knew he was in danger quite suddenly and with total certainty. What was happening had nothing to do with Cornwall and his surfing holiday. His other life, his life with MI6, had caught up with him. He remembered being chased down the mountainside at Point Blanc and knew that the same thing was happening again. Who or why didn't matter. He had just seconds to do something before the jet ski ran him down.

He flicked his head and saw it for just a second. A black nose like a torpedo. Gleaming chrome and glass. A man squatting low over the controls, his eyes fixed on Alex. The eyes were filled with hatred. They were less than a metre away.

There was only one thing Alex could do and he did it instantly, without thinking. The aerial is a move that demands split-second timing and total confidence. Alex twisted round and projected himself off the top of the wave and out into the air. At the same time, he crouched down and seized hold of the thruster, one hand on each side. Now he really was flying, suspended in mid-air as the wave rolled away beneath him. He saw the jet ski race past, covering the area where he had been only seconds before. He spun round, drawing an almost complete circle in the air. At the last moment, he remembered to place his foot right in the centre of the board. This would take all his weight when he landed.

The water rushed up to meet him. Alex finished his circle and plunged once again onto the face of the wave. It was a perfect landing. Water exploded around him but he remained upright and now he was just behind the jet ski. The rider turned back and Alex saw the look of astonishment on his face. The man was Chinese. Impossibly, incredibly, he was holding a gun. Alex saw it come up, water dripping off the barrel. This time there was nowhere he could go. He didn't have the strength to try another aerial. With a shout, he threw himself off the board and forward, onto the jet ski. He felt a jolt, his leg almost being pulled off as his board was torn away by the suddenly malevolent water.

There was an explosion. The man had fired. But the bullet missed. Alex thought he felt it pass over his shoulder. At the same moment, his hands grabbed the man's throat. His knees crashed into the side of the jet ski. And then the entire world was whipped away as man and machine lost control and tumbled into a spinning vortex of water. Alex's leg jerked a second time and he felt the leash snap. He heard a shout. Suddenly the man wasn't there any more. Alex was on his own. He couldn't breathe. Water pounded down on him. He felt himself being sucked helplessly into it. He couldn't struggle. His arms and legs were useless. He had no strength left. He opened his mouth to scream and the water rushed in.

Then his shoulder hit something hard and he knew he had reached the bottom of the sea and that this would have to be his grave. He had dared to play with the Cribber and the Cribber had taken its revenge. Somewhere, far above, another wave broke over him, but Alex didn't see it. He lay where he was, finally at peace.

TWO WEEKS IN THE SUN

Alex wasn't sure what was more surprising. To be still alive, or to find himself back in the London headquarters of the Special Operations division of MI6.

The fact that he was still breathing was, he knew, entirely down to Sabina. She had been sitting on the beach, watching in awe as he rode the Cribber towards her. She had seen the jet ski coming up behind him even before he did and had known instinctively that something was wrong. She had started running the moment Alex had leapt into the air and was already in the water by the time he crashed down next to the jet ski and then disappeared below the surface. Later on, she would say that there had been a collision ... a terrible accident. From that distance, it was impossible to see what had really taken place.

Sabina was a strong swimmer and luck was on her side. Although the water was murky and the waves still huge, she knew where Alex had gone down and she was there in less than a minute. She found him on her third dive, dragged his unconscious body to the surface and then pulled him ashore. She had learned mouth-to-mouth resuscitation at school and she used that knowledge now, pressing her lips against his, forcing the air into his lungs. Even then, she was sure that Alex was dead. He wasn't breathing. His eyes were closed. Sabina pounded on his chest – once, twice – and was finally rewarded with a sudden spasm and a fit of coughing as Alex came to. By then, some of the other surfers had arrived. One of them had a mobile phone and called for an ambulance. There was no sign of the man on the jet ski.

Alex had been lucky too. As it turned out, he had ridden the Cribber just far enough to be near the end of its journey, when the wave had been at its weakest. A ton of water had fallen onto him, but five seconds earlier and it might have been ten tons. Also, he hadn't been too far from the shore when Sabina found him. Any further out and she might never have found him at all.

Five days had passed since then.

It was Monday morning, the start of a new week. Alex was sitting in room 1605, on the sixteenth floor of the anonymous building in Liverpool Street. He had sworn that he would never return here. The man and the woman with him in the room were the last two people he wanted to see. And yet here he was. He had been drawn in as easily as a fish in a net.

As usual, Alan Blunt didn't seem particularly pleased to see him, preferring to study the file on the desk in front of him rather than the boy himself. It was the fifth or sixth time Alex had met the man in overall command of this section of MI6 and he still knew almost nothing about him. Blunt was about fifty, a man in a suit in an office. He didn't seem to smoke and Alex couldn't imagine him drinking either. Was he married? Did he have children? Did he spend his weekends walking in the park or fishing or watching football matches? Somehow Alex doubted it. He wondered if Blunt had any existence at all outside these four walls. He was a man defined by his work. His whole life was devoted to secrets, and in the end his own life had become a secret itself.

He looked up from the neatly printed report.

"Crawley had no right to involve you in this business," he said.

Alex said nothing. For once, he wasn't sure that he disagreed.

"The Wimbledon tennis championships. You nearly got yourself killed." He glanced quizzically at Alex. "And this business in Cornwall. I don't like my agents getting involved in dangerous sports."

"I'm not one of your agents," Alex said.

"There's enough danger in the job without adding to it," Blunt went on, ignoring him. "What happened to the man on the jet ski?" he asked.

"We're interrogating him now," Mrs Jones replied.

The deputy head of Special Operations was wearing a grey trouser suit, with a black leather handbag that matched her eyes. There was a silver brooch on her lapel, shaped like a miniature dagger. It seemed appropriate.

She had been the first to visit Alex as he'd recovered in hospital in Newquay and she at least had been concerned about what had happened. Of course, she had shown little or no emotion. If anyone had asked, she would have said that she didn't want to lose someone who had been useful to her and who might be useful again. But Alex suspected this was only half the story. She was a woman and he was fourteen years old. If Mrs Jones had a son, he could well be the same age as Alex. That made a difference – one that she wasn't quite able to ignore.

"We found a tattoo on the man's arm," she continued. "It seems that he was also a member of the Big Circle gang." She turned to Alex. "The Big Circle is a relatively new triad," she explained. "It's also, unfortunately, one of the most violent."

"I think I'd noticed," Alex said.

"The man you knocked out and refrigerated at Wimbledon was a *Sai-lo*. That means 'little brother'. You have to understand how these people work. You smashed their operation and made them lose face. That's the last thing they can afford. So they sent someone after you. He hasn't said anything yet but we believe he's a *Dai-lo*, or a 'big brother'. He'll have a rank of 438 ... that's one under the Dragon Head, the leader of the triad. And now he's failed too. It's a little unfortunate, Alex, that as well as half-drowning him, you also broke his nose. The triad will take that as another humiliation."

"I didn't do anything," Alex said. It was true. He remembered how the thruster had finally been torn away from his ankle. It wasn't his fault that it had hit the man in the face.

"That's not how they'll see it," Mrs Jones went on. She sounded like a schoolteacher. "What we're dealing with here is *Guan-shi*."

Alex waited for her to explain.

"*Guan-shi* is what gives Big Circle its power," she said. "It's a system of mutual respect. It ties all the members together. It essentially means that if you hurt one of them, you hurt them all. And if one of them becomes your enemy, they all do."

"You attack one of their people at Wimbledon," Blunt rasped, "they send another down to Cornwall."

"You take out their man in Cornwall, the order goes out to the other members of the triad to kill you," Mrs Jones said.

"How many other members are there?" Alex asked.

"About nineteen thousand at the last count," Blunt replied.

There was a long silence, punctured only by the distant traffic sixteen floors below.

"Every minute you stay in this country, you're in danger," Mrs Jones said. "And there's not a great deal we can do. Of course, we have some influence with the triads. If we let the right people know that you're protected by us, it may be possible to call them off. But that's going to take time and the fact of the matter is, they're probably working on the next plan of attack right now."

"You can't go home," Blunt said. "You can't go back to school. You can't go anywhere on your own. That woman who looks after you, the house-keeper, we've already arranged for her to be sent out of London. We can't take any chances."

"So what am I meant to do?" Alex asked.

Mrs Jones glanced at Blunt, who nodded. Neither of them looked particularly concerned and he suddenly realized that things had worked out exactly as they wanted. Somehow, without knowing it, he had played right into their hands.

"By coincidence, Alex," Mrs Jones began, "a few days ago we had a request for your services. It came from an American intelligence service. The Central Intelligence Agency – or CIA as you probably know them. They need a young person for an operation they happen to be mounting and they wondered if you might be available."

Alex was surprised. MI6 had used him twice and both times they had stressed that nobody was to know. Now, it seemed, they had been boasting about their teenage spy. Worse than that, they had even been preparing to lend him out, like a library book.

As if reading his mind, Mrs Jones raised a hand. "We had told them, of course, that you had no wish to continue in this line of work," she said. "That was, after all, what you had told us. A schoolboy, not a spy. That's what you said. But it does seem now that everything has changed. I'm sorry, Alex, but for whatever reason, you've chosen to go back into the field and unfortunately you're in danger. You have to disappear. This might be the best way."

"You want me to go to America?" Alex asked.

"Not exactly America," Blunt cut in. "We want you to go to Cuba ... or, at least, to an island just a few miles south of Cuba. It's called Cayo Esqueleto. That's Spanish. It means—"

"Skeleton Key," Alex said.

"That's right. Of course, there are plenty of keys off the coast of America. You'll have heard of Key Largo and Key West. This one was discovered by Sir Francis Drake. The story goes that when he landed there, the place was uninhabited. But he found a single skeleton, a conquistador in full armour, sitting on the beach. That was how the island got its name. Anyway, no matter what it's called, it's actually a very beautiful place. A tourist resort. Luxury hotels, diving, sailing... We're not asking you to do anything dangerous, Alex. Quite the contrary. You can think of this as a paid holiday. Two weeks in the sun."

"Go on," Alex said. He couldn't help sounding doubtful.

"The CIA is interested in Cayo Esqueleto because of a man who lives there. He's a Russian. He has a huge house – some might even call it a palace – on a sort of isthmus, that is to say, a narrow strip of land at the very northern tip of the island. His name is General Alexei Sarov."

Blunt pulled a photograph out of the file and turned it round so that Alex could see. It showed a fit-looking man in military uniform. The picture had been taken in Red Square, Moscow. Alex could see the onion-shaped towers of the Kremlin behind him.

"Sarov belongs to a different age," Mrs Jones said, taking over. "He was a commander in the Russian army at a time when the Russians were our enemies and still part of the Soviet Union. This wasn't very long ago, Alex. The collapse of communism. It was only in 1989 that the Berlin Wall came down." She stopped. "I suppose none of this means very much to you."

"Well, it wouldn't," Alex said. "I was only two years old."

"Yes, of course. But you have to understand, Sarov was a hero of the old Russia. He was made a general when he was only thirty-eight – the same year that his country invaded Afghanistan. He fought there for ten years, rising to be second in command of the Red Army. He had a son who was killed there. Sarov didn't even go the funeral. It would have meant abandoning his men and he wouldn't do that – not even for one day."

Alex looked at the photograph again. He could see the hardness in the man's eyes. It was a face without a shred of warmth.

"The war in Afghanistan ended when the Soviets withdrew in 1989," Mrs Jones continued. "At the same time, the whole country was falling apart. Communism came to an end and Sarov left. He made no secret of the fact that he didn't like the new Russia with its jeans and Nike trainers and McDonald's on every street corner. He left the army, although he still calls himself General, and went to live—"

"In Skeleton Key." Alex finished the sentence.

"Yes. He's been there for ten years now – and this is the point, Alex. In two weeks' time, the Russian president is planning to meet him there.

There's nothing surprising in that. The two men are old friends. They even grew up in the same part of Moscow. But the CIA are worried. They want to know what Sarov is up to. Why are the two men meeting? Old Russia and new Russia. What's going on?"

"The CIA want to spy on Sarov."

"Yes. It's a simple surveillance operation. They want to send in an undercover team to take a look around before the president arrives."

"Fine." Alex shrugged. "But why do they need me?"

"Because Skeleton Key is a communist island," Blunt explained. "It belongs to Cuba, one of the last places in the western world where communism still exists. Getting in and out of the place is extremely difficult. There's an airport at Santiago. But every plane is watched. Every passenger is checked. They're always on the lookout for American spies and anyone who is even slightly suspect is stopped and turned away."

"And that's why the CIA have come to us," Mrs Jones continued. "A single man might be suspicious. A man and a woman might be a team. But a man and a woman travelling with a child...? That has to be a family!"

"That's all they want from you, Alex," Blunt

said. "You go in with them. You stay at their hotel. You swim, snorkel and enjoy the sun. They do all the work. You're only there as part of their cover."

"Couldn't they use an American boy?" Alex asked.

Blunt coughed, obviously embarrassed. "The Americans would never use one of their own young people in an exercise like this," he said. "They have a different set of rules to us."

"You mean they'd be worried about getting him killed."

"We wouldn't have asked you, Alex," Mrs Jones broke the awkward silence. "But you have to leave London. In fact, you have to leave England. We're not trying to get you killed. We're trying to protect you and this is the best way. Mr Blunt is right. Cayo Esqueleto is a beautiful island and you're really very lucky to be going there. You can look on the whole thing as a free holiday."

Alex thought it over. He looked from Alan Blunt to Mrs Jones, but of course they were giving nothing away. How many agents had sat in this room with the two of them, listening to their honeyed words?

It's a simple job. Nothing to it. You'll be back in two weeks...

His own uncle had been one of them, sent to check on security in a computer factory on the south coast. But Ian Rider had never made it back.

Alex wanted none of it. There were still a few weeks of the summer holidays left and he wanted to see Sabina again. The two of them had talked about northern France and the Loire Valley, youth hostels and hiking. He had friends in London. Jack Starbright, his housekeeper and closest friend, had offered to take him with her when she visited her parents in Chicago. Seven weeks of normality. Was it too much to ask?

And yet, he remembered what had happened on the Cribber when the man on the jet ski had caught up with him. Alex had seen his eyes for just a few seconds but there had been no mistaking their cruelty and fanaticism. This was a man who had been prepared to chase him across the top of a twenty-foot wave in order to mow him down from behind – and he had come perilously close to succeeding. Alex knew, with a sick certainty, that the triad would try again. He had offended them ... not once now, but twice. Blunt was right about that. Any hope of an ordinary summer had gone out the window.

"If I help your friends in the CIA, you can get

the triad to leave me alone?" he asked.

Mrs Jones nodded. "We have contacts in the Chinese underworld. But it will take time, Alex. Whatever happens, you're going to have to go into hiding – at least for the next couple of weeks."

So why not do it in the sun?

Alex nodded wearily. "All right," he said. "It seems I don't really have a lot of choice. When do you want me to leave?"

Blunt took an envelope out of the file. "I have your air ticket here," he said. "There's a flight this afternoon."

Of course, they had known he would accept.

"We will want to keep in touch with you while you're away," Mrs Jones muttered.

"I'll send you a postcard," Alex said.

"No, Alex, that's not quite what I had in mind. Why don't you go and have a word with Smithers?"

Smithers had an office on the eleventh floor of the building and at first Alex had to admit he was disappointed.

It was Smithers who had designed the various gadgets Alex had used on his previous missions and Alex had expected to find him somewhere in the basement, surrounded by cars and motorbikes, hi-tech weapons and men and women in white coats. But this room was boring: large, square and anonymous. It could have belonged to the chief executive of almost anything; an insurance company, perhaps, or a bank. There was a steel and glass desk with a telephone, a computer, "in" and "out" trays and an anglepoise lamp. A leather sofa stood against one wall, and on the other side of the room was a silver filing cabinet with six drawers. A picture hung on the wall behind the desk; a view of the sea. But disappointingly, there were no gadgets anywhere. Not so much as an electric pencil sharpener.

Smithers himself was behind the desk, tapping at the computer with fingers almost too big for the keys. He was one of the fattest people Alex had ever met. Today he was wearing a black three-piece suit with what looked like an old school tie perched limply on the great bulge of his stomach. Seeing Alex, he stopped typing and swivelled round in a leather chair that must have been reinforced to take his weight.

"My dear boy!" he exclaimed. "How delightful to see you. Come in, come in! How have you been keeping? I hear you had a bit of trouble, that business in France. You really must look after yourself, Alex. I'd be mortified if anything happened to you. Door!"

Alex was surprised when the door swung shut behind him.

"Voice activated," Smithers explained. "Do, please, sit down."

Alex sat on a second leather chair on the other side of the desk. As he did so, there was a low hum and the anglepoise lamp swivelled round and bent towards him like some sort of metallic bird taking a closer look. At the same time, the computer screen flickered and a human skeleton appeared. Alex moved a hand. The skeleton's hand moved. With a shudder, he realized he was looking at – or rather, through – himself.

"You're looking well," Smithers said. "Good bone structure!"

"What...?" Alex began.

"It's just something I've been working on. A simple X-ray device. Useful if anyone is wearing a gun." Smithers pressed a button and the screen went blank. "Now, Mr Blunt tells me that you're off to join our friends in the CIA. They're fine operators. Very, very good – except, of course, you can never trust them and they have no sense of humour. Cayo Esqueleto, I understand...?"

He leant forward and pressed another button on the desk. Alex glanced at the painting on the wall. The waves had begun to move! At the same time, the image shifted, pulling back, and he realized that he was looking at a plasma television screen with a picture beamed by satellite from somewhere above the Atlantic Ocean. Alex found himself looking down on an irregularly shaped island surrounded by turquoise water. The image was time coded and he realized that it was being broadcast into the room live.

"Tropical climate," Smithers muttered. "There'll be quite a lot of rainfall at this time of year. I've been developing a poncho that doubles as a parachute, but I don't think you'll need that. And I've got a marvellous mosquito coil. As a matter of fact, mosquitoes are about the only thing it *won't* knock out. But you won't need that either! In fact, I'm told the only thing you actually do need is something to help you keep in touch."

"A secret transmitter," Alex said.

"Why does it have to be secret?" Smithers pulled open a drawer and took out an object which he placed in front of Alex.

It was a mobile phone.

"I've already got one, thanks," Alex muttered.

"Not one like this," Smithers retorted. "It gives you a direct link with this office, even when you're in America. It works underwater – and in space. The pads are fingerprint sensitive so only you can use it. This is the model five. We also have a model seven. You hold it upside down when you dial or it blows up in your hand—"

"Why can't I have that model?" Alex asked.

"Mr Blunt has forbidden it." Smithers leant forward conspiratorially. "But I have put in a little extra for you. You see the aerial just here? Dial 999 and it'll shoot out like a needle. Drugged, of course. It'll knock out anyone in a twenty metre range."

"Right." Alex picked up the phone. "Have you got anything else?"

"I was told you weren't to have any weapons..." Smithers sighed, then leant forward and spoke into a potted plant. "Could you bring them up, please, Miss Pickering?"

Alex was beginning to have serious doubts about this office – and these were confirmed a moment later when the leather sofa suddenly split in half, the two ends moving away from each other. At the same time, part of the floor slid aside to allow another piece of sofa to shoot silently into place, turning the two-seater into a three-seater. A young woman had been carried up with the new piece. She was sitting with her legs crossed and her hands on her knee. She stood up and walked over to Smithers.

"These are the items you requested," she said, handing over a package. She produced a sheet of paper and placed it in front of him. "And this report just came in from Cairo."

"Thank you, Miss Pickering."

Smithers waited until the woman had left – using the door this time – then glanced quickly at the report. "Not good news," he muttered. "Not good news at all. Oh well..." He slid the report into the "out" tray. There was a flash of electricity as the paper self-destructed. A second later, there were only ashes left. "I'm bending the rules doing this," he went on. "But there were a couple of things I'd been developing for you and I don't see why you shouldn't take them with you. Better safe than sorry."

He turned the package upside down and a bright pink packet of bubblegum slid out. "The fun of working with you, Alex," Smithers said, "is adapting the things you'd expect to find in the pockets of a boy your age. And I'm extremely pleased with this one."

"Bubblegum?"

"It blows rather special bubbles. Chew it for thirty seconds and the chemicals in your saliva react with the compound, making it expand. And as it expands, it'll shatter just about anything. Put it in a gun, for example, and it'll crack it open. Or the lock on a door."

Alex turned the packet over. Written in yellow letters on the side was the word BUBBLE 0-7. "What flavour did you make it?" he asked.

"Strawberry. Now, this other device is even more dangerous and I'm sure you won't need it. I call it the Striker and I'd be very happy to have it back."

Smithers shook the package and a keyring slid out to join the bubblegum on the desk. It had a plastic figurine attached, a footballer wearing white shorts and a red shirt. Alex leant forward and turned it over. He found himself looking at a three centimetre high model of Michael Owen.

"Thanks, Mr Smithers," he said. "But personally I've never supported Liverpool."

"This is the prototype. We can always do another footballer next time. The important thing is the head. Remember this, Alex. Twist it round twice clockwise and once anti-clockwise and you'll arm the device."

"It'll explode?"

"It's a stun grenade. Flash and a bang. A ten second fuse. Not powerful enough to kill – but in a confined space it will incapacitate the opposition for a couple of minutes, which might give you a chance to get away."

Alex pocketed the Michael Owen figure and the bubblegum along with the mobile telephone. He stood up, feeling more confident. This might be a simple surveillance operation, a paid holiday as Blunt had put it, but he still didn't want to go empty-handed.

"Good luck, Alex," Smithers said. "I hope you get on all right with the CIA. They're not really like us, you know. And heaven knows what they'll make of you."

"I'll see you, Mr Smithers."

"I've got a private lift if you're going downstairs." As Smithers spoke, the six drawers of the filing cabinet slid open, three going one way, three going the other, to reveal a brightly lit cubicle behind.

Alex shook his head. "Thanks, Mr Smithers," he said. "I'll take the stairs."

"Whatever you say, old boy. Just look after yourself. And whatever you do, don't swallow the gum!"

NOT SO SPECIAL AGENTS

Alex stood at the window, trying to make sense of the world in which he now found himself. Seven hours on a plane had drained something out of him which even the surprise of a seat in first class had been unable to put back. He felt disengaged, as if his body had managed to arrive but had left half his brain somewhere behind.

He was looking at the Atlantic Ocean. It was on the other side of a strip of dazzling white sand that stretched into the distance with loungers and umbrellas laid out like measurements on a ruler. Miami was at the southernmost tip of the United States of America and it seemed that half the people who came to the city had simply followed the sun. He could see hundreds of them, lying on their backs in the tiniest of bikinis and swimming trunks, thighs and biceps pounded to perfection in the gym and then brought out to roast. Sun worshippers? No. These people were here because they worshipped themselves.

It was late afternoon and the heat was still intense. But in England, eight thousand kilometres away, it was night – and Alex was struggling to stay awake. He was also cold. The air-conditioning in the building had been turned up to maximum. The sun might be shining on the other side of the glass but in this neat, expensive office, he was chilled. Miami Ice, he thought.

It hadn't been the welcome he had expected. There had been a driver waiting for him when he arrived at the airport, a heavy-set man in a suit with Alex's name on a card. The man was wearing sunglasses that obliterated his eyes, offering Alex two reflections of himself.

"You Rider?"

"Yes."

"The car's this way."

The car turned out to be a stretch limousine. Alex felt ridiculous sitting alone in a long, narrow compartment with two leather seats facing each other, a drinks cabinet and a TV screen. It was nothing like a car at all, and he was glad that the windows, like the driver's glasses, were darkened.

Nobody would be able to see in. He watched as the shops and boatyards on the airport perimeter slipped past and then they were suddenly crossing the water on a wide causeway that skimmed across the bay towards Miami Beach. Now the buildings were low-rise, barely taller than the palm trees that surrounded them, and painted astonishing shades of pink and pale blue. The roads were wide, but more people seemed to be sweeping half-naked down the centre line on roller blades than driving.

The limousine stopped outside a ten-storey white building with lines so sharp it could have been cut out of a giant sheet of paper. There was a coffee bar on the ground floor, with offices up above. Leaving Alex's cases in the car, they went in through the lobby and took the lift (elevator, Alex reminded himself) up to the tenth. It opened directly onto the reception area of what looked like an ordinary office, with two efficient girls behind a curving mahogany desk. A sign read: CENTURION INTERNATIONAL ADVERTIZING. CIA, Alex thought. Great!

"Alex Rider for Mr Byrne," the driver said.

"This way." One of the girls gestured at a door to one side. Alex wouldn't even have noticed it otherwise.

Everything was different on the other side of the reception area.

Alex was confronted by two glass tubes with two sliding doors – one in, one out. The driver gestured and he stepped inside. The door closed automatically and there was a hum as he was scanned – for both conventional and biological weapons, he guessed. Then the door opened on the other side and he followed the driver down a blank, empty corridor and into an office.

"I hope you don't feel homesick, so far away from England."

The driver had gone and Alex was alone with another man, this one aged about sixty, with grizzled white hair and a moustache. He looked fit, but he moved slowly, as if he had just got out of bed or needed to get into it. He was wearing a dark suit that looked out of place in Miami, a white shirt and a knitted tie. His name was Joe Byrne and he was the deputy director for operations in the Covert Action section of the CIA.

"No," Alex said, "I feel fine." This wasn't true. He was already wishing he hadn't come. He would have liked to be back in London, even if it had meant hiding from the triads somehow. But he wasn't going to tell Byrne that.

"You have quite a reputation," Byrne said.

"Do I?"

"You bet." Byrne smiled. "Dr Grief and that guy in England – Herod Sayle. Don't worry, Alex! We're not meant to know about these things but these days ... nothing happens in the world without someone hearing about it. You can't cough in Kabul without someone recording it in Washington." He smiled to himself. "I have to hand it to you Brits. Here at the CIA, we've used cats and dogs – we tried to put a cat into the Korean embassy with a bug in its collar. It was a neat operation and it would have worked, but unfortunately they ate it. But we've never used a kid before. Certainly not a kid like you..."

Alex shrugged. He knew Byrne was trying to be friendly, but at the same time the old man was uneasy and it showed.

"You've done some great work for your country," Byrne concluded.

"I'm not sure I did it for my country," Alex said. "It's just that my country didn't give me a lot of choice."

"Well, we're really grateful you've agreed to help us now. You know, the United States and Great Britain have always had a special relationship. We like to help each other." There was an awkward silence. "I met your uncle once," Byrne said. "Ian Rider."

"He was here in Miami?"

"No. It was in Washington. He was a good man, Alex. A good agent. I was sorry to hear—"

"Thanks," Alex said.

Byrne coughed. "You must be tired. We've booked you a hotel just a few blocks from here. But first I want you to meet special agents Turner and Troy. They should be here any moment."

Turner and Troy. They were going to be Alex's mother and father. He wondered which one was which.

"Anyway, the three of you will be leaving for Cayo Esqueleto the day after tomorrow," Byrne said. He sat down on the arm of a chair. His eyes had never left Alex. "You need a bit of time to get over your jet-lag and, more importantly, you need to get to know your new mum and dad." He hesitated. "I should mention to you, Alex, that they weren't too crazy about your part in this operation. Don't get me wrong. They know you're a pretty smart operator. But you *are* fourteen."

"Fourteen and three months," Alex said.

"Yeah. Sure." Byrne wasn't sure if Alex was serious. "Obviously, they're not used to having young people like you around when they're in the field. It bugs them. But they'll get used to it.

And the main thing is, once you've helped get them onto the island, you'll be able to keep out of their way. I'm sure Alan Blunt told you – just stay in the hotel and enjoy yourself. The whole thing should only take a week. Two weeks, tops."

"What exactly are they hoping to achieve?" Alex asked.

"Well, they need to get into the Casa de Oro. That's Spanish. It means 'golden house'. It's an old plantation house that General Sarov has at one end of the island. But it's not going to be easy, Alex. The island narrows and there's a single track road with water on either side leading up to the outer wall. The place itself is more like a castle than a house. Anyway, that's not your problem. We have people on the island who can help us find a way in. And once we get in we can bug the place. We have cameras the size of a pin!"

"You want to know what General Sarov is doing."

"Exactly." Byrne glanced down at his brightly polished shoes and suddenly Alex wondered if the CIA man was keeping something from him. It all sounded too straightforward – and what had Smithers said? *You can never trust them*. Byrne seemed pleasant enough, but now he wondered.

There was a knock on the door. Without waiting for an answer, a man and woman walked in.

Byrne stood up. "Alex," he said, "I'd like you to meet Tom Turner and Belinda Troy. People ... this is Alex Rider."

The atmosphere in the room became icy in an instant. Alex had never met two people less pleased to see him.

Tom Turner was about forty, a handsome man, with fair, close-cropped hair, blue eyes and a face that managed to be both tough and boyish. He was dressed – strangely – in jeans, a white open-necked shirt and a loose, soft leather jacket. There was nothing wrong with the clothes. They just didn't seem to suit him. This was a man who had been moulded by the work he did. With his clean-shaven, rather plastic looks, he reminded Alex of a dummy in a shop window. Turn him over, Alex thought, and you'd find CIA stamped on the soles of his feet.

Belinda Troy was a couple of years older than him, slim, with brown frizzy hair tumbling down to her shoulders. She was also casually dressed in a loose-fitting skirt and T-shirt, with a brightly coloured bag dangling from her shoulder and a loose string of beads around her neck. She didn't seem to be wearing any make-up. Her lips were pressed tightly together. Not quite scowling, but still a hundred miles away from a smile. She reminded Alex of a schoolteacher ... maybe one in a nursery school. Troy closed the door and sat down. Somehow she had managed to avoid looking at Alex from the moment she had entered the room. It was as if she was trying to pretend he wasn't there.

Alex looked from one to the other. The strange thing was that despite their appearances, there was something identical about Tom Turner and Belinda Troy. It was as if they had both survived the same, bad accident. They were hard-bitten, emotionless, empty. Now he knew why the CIA needed him. If they'd tried to get these two into Skeleton Key on their own, they'd have been identified as spies before they'd even got off the plane.

"It's nice to meet you, Alex," Turner said in a way that made it sound quite the opposite.

"How was the flight?" Troy asked. And then, before Alex could answer. "I guess it must have been scary. Travelling on your own."

"I had to close my eyes during take-off," Alex said. "But I stopped trembling when we got to thirty-five thousand feet."

"You're scared of flying?" Turner was astonished.

"That's crazy!" Troy turned to Byrne. "You're putting this kid into a CIA operation and already we find out he's scared of flying!"

"No, no, Belinda! Tom!" Byrne was embarrassed. "I think Alex was joking."

"Joking?"

"That's right. He's just got a different sense of humour."

Troy was tight-lipped. "Well, I don't find it funny," she said. "In fact, I think this whole idea is crazy. I'm sorry, sir..." she went on quickly, before Byrne could interrupt her. "You tell me this boy has a reputation. But he's still a minor! Suppose he makes a dumb-ass joke when we're in the field? He could blow our cover! And what about that accent of his? You're not going to tell me he's American?"

"He doesn't sound American," Turner agreed.

"Alex won't need to talk," Byrne said. "And if he does, I'm sure he can put on an accent."

Turner coughed. "Permission to speak, sir?"

"Go ahead, Turner."

"I agree one hundred per cent with special agent Troy, sir. I've got nothing against Alex. But he's not trained. He's not tested. He's not American!"

"Goddammit!" Suddenly Byrne was angry. "We've been through all this. You know how tough security is on the island – and with the Russian president on the way, it's going to be worse than ever. You go into Santiago airport on your own and you won't make it out the other side. Remember what happened to Johnson! He went in on his own, dressed up as a birdwatcher. That was three months ago and we haven't heard from him since!"

"Well find us an American kid!"

"That's enough, Turner. Alex has flown thousands of miles to help us and I think you could at least show a little appreciation. Both of you. Alex..." Byrne gestured at Alex to sit down. "Can I get you anything? You want a drink? A Coke?"

"I'm fine," Alex said, and sat down.

Byrne opened a drawer in his desk and took out a bundle of papers and official documents. Alex recognized the green cover of an American passport. "Now this is how we're going to work it," he began. "The first thing is, all three of you are going to need fake IDs when you go into Cayo Esqueleto. I thought it would be easier to keep your first names – so it's Alex Gardiner who's going to be travelling with his mum and dad, Tom and Belinda Gardiner. Look after these documents, by the way. The agency is prohibited from manufacturing false passports and I had to pull strings to get hold of them. When this is over, I want them back."

Alex opened the passport. He was amazed to

find his own photograph already in place. His age was the same, but according to the passport he had been born in California. He wondered how it had been done. And when.

"You live in Los Angeles," Byrne explained. "You're at high school in west Hollywood. Your dad's in the movie business and this is a week's vacation to do some diving and see the sights. I'll give you some stuff to read tonight, and of course everything's been backstopped."

"What does that mean?" Alex asked.

"It means that if anyone asks anything about the Gardiner family living in LA, it'll all check out. The school, the neighbourhood, everything. There are people out there who'll say they've known you all your life." Byrne paused. "Listen, Alex. You have to understand. The United States of America is not at war with Cuba. Sure, we've had our differences, but for the most part we've managed to live side by side. But they do things their way. Cuba – and that means Cayo Esqueleto – is a country in its own right. They find you're a spy, they're going to put you in jail. They're going to interrogate you. Maybe they'll kill you – and there's nothing we can do to stop them. It's been three months since we heard from Johnson and my gut feeling is we're never going to hear from him again."

There was a long silence.

Byrne realized he'd gone too far. "But nothing's going to happen to you," he said. "You're not part of this operation. You're just watching from the sideline." He turned to the two agents. "The important thing is to start acting like a unit. You only have two days until you leave. That means spending time together. I guess Alex will be too tired for dinner tonight but you can start by having breakfast together tomorrow. Spend the day together. Start thinking like a family. That's what you've got to be."

It was strange. Lying in bed in Cornwall, Alex had wished he could belong to a family. And now the wish had come true – though not in the way he had intended.

"Any questions?" Byrne asked.

"Yes, sir. I have a question," Turner said. He was sulking. His mouth had become little more than a straight line quickly drawn across his handsome face. "You want us to play happy families tomorrow. OK, sir, if that's an order, I'll do my best. But I think you're forgetting that tomorrow I'm meant to be seeing the Salesman. I don't think he'll be expecting me to turn up with my wife and child."

"The Salesman?" Byrne was annoyed.

"I'm seeing him at midday."

"What about Troy?"

"I'll be there as back-up," Troy said. "This is standard procedure—"

"All right!" Byrne thought for a moment. "The Salesman is on the water, right? Turner – you'll go onto the boat. So Alex can stay with Troy, on land. Safely out of the way."

Byrne stood up. The meeting was over. Alex felt another wave of tiredness surge through him and had to fight off a yawn. Byrne must have noticed. "You get some rest, Alex," he said. "I'm sure you and I will meet again. And I really am grateful you've agreed to help." He held out a hand. Alex shook it.

But special agent Troy was still sullen. "We'll have breakfast at ten-thirty," she said. "That'll give you time to read all the paperwork. Not that you'll probably sleep that much anyway. Where are you staying?"

Alex shrugged.

"I've put him up at the Delano," Byrne said.

"OK. We'll pick you up there."

Turner and Troy turned round and left the room. Neither of them bothered to say goodbye.

"Don't mind them," Byrne said. "This is a new situation for them. But they're good agents. Turner entered the military straight after college and Troy has worked with him many times before. They'll look after you when you're out in the field. I'm sure everything will work out fine."

But somehow Alex doubted it. And he was still puzzled. A lot of work, a lot of thought had gone into this operation. False papers – with his photograph – had been prepared before he had even known he was coming. A whole identity had been set up for him in Los Angeles. And another agent, Johnson, had possibly died.

A simple surveillance operation? Byrne was nervous. Alex was sure of it. Maybe Turner and Troy were too.

Whatever was happening on Skeleton Key, they weren't telling him the full truth. Somehow, he'd have to find that out for himself.

It was a room that didn't really look like a room at all. It was too big. It had too many doors – and not just doors but archways, alcoves and a wide terrace open to the sun. The floor was marble, a chessboard of green and white squares that seemed somehow to exaggerate its size. The furniture was ornate, antique – and it was everywhere. Highly polished tables and chairs. Pedestals with vases and statuettes. Huge, gold-framed mirrors. Spectacular chandeliers. A giant stuffed crocodile lay in front of a massive fireplace. The man who had killed it sat opposite.

General Sarov was sipping black coffee out of a tiny porcelain cup. Caffeine is addictive and Sarov allowed himself only one thimbleful of coffee once a day. It was his single vice and he savoured it. Today he was dressed in a casual linen suit, but on this man it looked almost formal, with not a crease in it. His shirt was open at the collar revealing a neck that could have been carved out of grey stone. A ceiling fan turned slowly, a few metres above the desk where he was sitting. Sarov savoured the last mouthful of coffee, then lowered the cup and saucer back onto his desk. The porcelain made no sound as it came to rest on the polished surface.

There was a knock at the door – one of the doors – and a man walked into the room. *Walked*, however, was the wrong word. There was no word to describe exactly how this man moved.

Everything about him was wrong. His head sat at an angle on shoulders which were themselves crooked and hunched. His right arm was shorter than his left arm. His right leg, however, was several centimetres longer than his left. His feet were encased in black leather shoes, one heavier and larger than the other. He was wearing a black leather jacket and jeans, and as he approached Sarov his muscles rippled beneath the cloth as if with a life of their own. Nothing in his body was co-ordinated, so although he was moving forwards, he seemed to be trying to go backwards or sideways. His face was the worst part of him. It was as if it had been taken to pieces and put back together again by a child with only a vague knowledge of the human form. There were about a dozen scars on his neck and around his cheeks. One of his eyes was red, permanently bloodshot. He had long, colourless hair on one half of his head. On the other, he was completely bald.

Although it would have been impossible to tell from looking at him, this man was only twenty-eight years old and, until a few years ago, had been the most feared terrorist in Europe. His name was Conrad. Very little was known about him, although it was said that he was Turkish, that he had been born in Istanbul, the son of a butcher, and that when he was nine he had blown up his school with a bomb made in chemistry class when he was given a detention for being late.

Again, nobody knew who had trained Conrad or, for that matter, who had employed him. He was a chameleon. He had no political beliefs and operated simply for money. It was believed that he had been responsible for outrages in Paris, Madrid, Athens and London. One thing was certain. The security services of nine different countries were after him, he was number four on the CIA's most wanted list, and there was an official bounty of two million dollars on his head.

His career had come to a sudden and unexpected end in the winter of 1998 when a bomb that he had been carrying – intended for an army base – had detonated early. The bomb had quite literally blown him apart, but it hadn't quite managed to kill him. He had been stitched back together by a team of Albanian doctors in a research centre near Elbasan. It was their handiwork that was so visible now.

He was working as Sarov's personal assistant and secretary. He had done so for two years. Such work would once have been beneath him but Conrad had little choice now. And anyway, he understood the scope of Sarov's vision. In the new world that the Russian intended to create, Conrad would have his rewards.

"Good morning, comrade," Sarov said. He spoke in fluent English. "I hope we've managed to recover the rest of the banknotes from the swamp."

Conrad nodded. He preferred not to speak.

"Excellent. The money will, of course, have to be laundered. Then it can be paid back into my account." Sarov reached out and opened a leather-bound diary. There were a number of entries, each one in perfect handwriting. "Everything is proceeding according to schedule," he went on. "The construction of the bomb...?"

"Complete." Conrad seemed to have difficulty getting the word out of his mouth. He had to twist his face to make it happen at all.

"I knew I could rely on you. The Russian president will be arriving here in just five days' time. I had an email from him confirming it today. Boris tells me how much he's looking forward to his holiday." Sarov smiled very briefly. "It will, of course, be a holiday that he is unlikely to forget. You have the rooms prepared?"

Conrad nodded.

"The cameras?"

"Yes, General."

"Good." Sarov ran a finger down the diary pages. He stopped at a single word that had been underlined with a question mark. "There still remains the question of the uranium," he said. "I always knew that the purchase and delivery of nuclear material would be dangerous and delicate. The men in the aircraft threatened me and they have paid the price. But they were, of course, working for a third party."

"The Salesman," Conrad said.

"Indeed. By now, the Salesman will have heard what happened to his messenger boys. When no further payment arrives from me, he may decide to go ahead with his threat and alert the authorities. It's unlikely, but it's still a risk I am not prepared to take. We have less than two weeks until the bomb is detonated and the world takes on the shape that I have decided to give it. We cannot take any chances. And so, my dear Conrad, you must go to Miami and remove the Salesman from our lives – which will, I fear, involve removing him from his."

"Where is he?"

"He operates out of a boat, a cruise liner called *Mayfair Lady*. It's usually moored at the Bayside Marketplace. The Salesman feels safer on the water. Speaking personally, I will feel safer when he is underneath it." Sarov closed the diary. The meeting was over. "You can leave straight away. Report to me when it is done."

Conrad nodded a third time. The metal pins in his neck rippled briefly as his head moved up and down. Then he turned round and walked, limped, *dragged* himself out of the room.

DEATH OF A SALESMAN

They had a late breakfast at a café in Bayside Marketplace, right on the quayside, with boats moored all around them and bright yellow and green water taxis nipping back and forth. Tom Turner and Belinda Troy had knocked on Alex's door at ten o'clock that morning. In fact, Alex had been awake for several hours. He had fallen asleep fast, slept heavily and woken too early – the classic pattern of trans-Atlantic jet-lag. But at least he'd had plenty of time to read through the papers that Joe Byrne had given him. He now knew everything about his new identity – the best friends he had never met, the pet dog he had never seen, even the high school grades he had never achieved.

And now he was sitting with his new mother

and father watching the tourists on the board-walk, strolling in and out of the pretty white-fronted boutiques that cluttered the area. The sun was already high, the glare coming off the water almost blinding. Alex slipped on a pair of Oakley Eye Jackets and the world on the other side of the black iridium lenses became softer and more manageable. The glasses had been a present from Jack. He hadn't expected to need them so soon.

There was a book of matches on the table with the words THE SNACKYARD printed on the cover. Alex picked it up and turned it over in his fingers. The matches were warm. He was surprised the sun hadn't set them alight. A waiter in black and white, complete with bow tie, came over to take the order. Alex glanced at the menu. He had never thought it possible to have so much choice for breakfast. At the next table a man was eating his way through a stack of pancakes with bacon, hash browns and scrambled eggs. Alex was hungry but the sight took away his own appetite.

"I'll just have some orange juice and toast," he said.

"Wholemeal or granary?"

"Granary. With butter and jam—"

"You mean *jelly*!" Troy paused until the waiter

had gone. "No American kid asks for jam." She scowled. "You ask for that at Santiago Airport and we'll be in jail – or worse – before you can blink."

"I wasn't thinking," Alex began.

"You don't think, you get killed. Worse, you get us killed." She shook her head. "I still say this is a bad idea."

"How's Lucky?" Turner asked.

Alex's head spun. What was he talking about? Then he remembered. Lucky was the Labrador dog that the Gardiner family was supposed to have back in Los Angeles. "He's fine," Alex said. "He's being looked after by Mrs Beach." She was the woman who lived next door.

But Turner wasn't impressed. "Not fast enough," he said. "If you have to stop to think about it, the enemy will know you're telling a lie. You have to talk about your dog and your neighbours as if you've known them all your life."

It wasn't fair, of course. Turner and Troy hadn't prepared him. He hadn't realized the test had already begun. In fact, this was the third time Alex had gone undercover with a new identity. He had been Felix Lester when he had been sent to Cornwall, and Alex Friend, the son of a multimillionaire, in the French Alps. Both times he had managed to play the part successfully and he knew that he could do it again now as Alex Gardiner.

"So how long have you been with the CIA?" Alex asked.

"That's classified information," Turner replied. He saw the look on Alex's face and softened. "All my life," he said. "I was in the marines. It's what I always wanted to do, even when I was a kid ... younger than you. I want to die for my country. That's my dream."

"We shouldn't be talking about ourselves," Belinda said angrily. "We're meant to be a family. So let's talk about the family!"

"All right, Mom," Alex muttered.

They asked him a few more questions about Los Angeles while they waited for the food to arrive. Alex answered on autopilot. He watched a couple of teenagers go past on skateboards and wished he could join them. That was what a fourteen year old should be doing in the Miami sunshine. Not playing spy games with two sour-faced adults who had already decided they weren't going to give him a chance.

The food came. Turner and Troy had both ordered fruit salad and cappuccino – decaffeinated with skimmed milk. Alex guessed they were watching their weight. His own toast came – with grape jelly. The butter was whipped and white and seemed to disappear when it was spread.

"So who is the Salesman?" Alex asked.

"You don't need to know that," Turner replied.

Alex decided he'd had enough. He put down his knife. "All right," he said. "You've made it pretty clear that you don't want to work with me. Well, that's fine, because I don't want to work with you either. And for what it's worth, nobody would ever believe you were my parents because no parents would ever behave like you two!"

"Alex—" Troy began.

"Forget it! I'm going back to London. And if your Mr Byrne asks why, you can tell him I didn't like the jelly so I went home to get some jam."

He stood up. Troy was on her feet at the same time. Alex glanced at Turner. He was looking uncertain too. He guessed that they would have been glad to see the back of him. But at the same time, they were afraid of their boss.

"Sit down, Alex," Troy said. She shrugged. "OK. We were out of line. We didn't mean to give you a hard time."

Alex met her eyes. He slowly sat down again.

"It's just gonna take us a bit of time to get used to the situation," Troy went on. "Turner and me ... we've worked together before ... but we don't know you."

Turner nodded. "You get killed, how's that gonna make us feel?"

"I was told there wasn't going to be any danger," Alex said. "Anyway, I can look after myself."

"I don't believe that."

Alex opened his mouth to speak, then stopped himself. There was no point arguing with these people. They'd already made up their minds, and anyway, they were the sort who were always right. He'd met teachers just like them. But at least he'd achieved something now. The two special agents had decided to loosen up.

"You want to know about the Salesman?" Troy began. "He's a crook. He's based here in Miami. He's a nasty piece of work."

"He's Mexican," Turner added. "From Mexico City."

"So what does he do?"

"He does just what his name says. He sells things. Drugs. Weapons. False identities. Information." Troy ticked off the list on her fingers. "If you need something and it's against the law, the Salesman will supply it. At a price, of course."

"I thought you were investigating Sarov."

"We are." Turner hesitated. "The Salesman may have sold something to Sarov. That's the connection."

"What did he sell?"

"We don't know for sure." Turner was looking increasingly nervous. "We just know that two of the Salesman's agents flew into Skeleton Key recently. They flew in but they didn't fly out again. We've been trying to find out what Sarov was buying."

"What's all this got to do with the Russian president?" Alex still wasn't sure he was being told the truth.

"We won't know that until we know what it was that Sarov bought," Troy said, as if explaining something to a six year old.

"I've been working undercover with the Salesman for a while now," Turner went on. "I'm buying drugs. Half a million dollars' worth of cocaine, being flown in from Colombia. At least, that's what he thinks." Turner smiled. "We have a pretty good relationship. He trusts me. And today just happens to be the Salesman's birthday, so he invited me to go for a drink on his boat."

Alex looked across to the sea. "Which one is it?"

"That one." Turner pointed at a boat moored at

the end of a jetty about fifty metres away. Alex drew a breath.

It was one of the most beautiful boats he had ever seen. Not sleek, white and fibreglass like so many of the cruisers he had seen moored around Miami. Not even modern. She was called *Mayfair Lady* and was an Edwardian classic motor yacht, eighty years old, like something out of a black and white film. The boat was one hundred and twenty feet long with a single funnel rising over its centre. The main saloon was at deck level, just behind the bridge. A sweeping line of fifteen or more portholes suggested cabins and dining rooms below. The boat was cream with natural wood trimmings, a wooden deck and brass lamps under the canopies. A tall, slender mast rose up at the front with a radar, the boat's one visible connection with the twenty-first century. *Mayfair Lady* didn't belong in Miami. She belonged in a museum. And every boat that came near her was somehow ugly by comparison.

"It's a nice boat," Alex said. "The Salesman must be doing well."

"The Salesman should be in jail," Troy muttered. She had seen the admiring look in Alex's eyes and didn't approve. "And one day that's where we're going to put him."

"Thirty years to life," Turner agreed.

Troy dug her spoon into her fruit salad. "All right, Alex," she said, "let's start again. Your maths teacher. What's her name?"

Alex looked round. "Her name is Mrs Hazeldene. And – nice try – but we learn *maths* in England. Americans learn *math*."

Troy nodded but didn't smile. "You're getting there," she said.

They finished their breakfast. The CIA agents tested Alex on a few more details, then lapsed into silence. They didn't ask him about his life in England, his friends, or how he had stumbled into the world of MI6. They didn't seem to want to know anything about him.

The skateboarders had stopped playing and were slumped on the boardwalk, drinking Cokes. Turner looked at his watch. "Time to go," he muttered.

"I'll stay with the kid," Troy said.

"I shouldn't be more than twenty minutes." Turner stood up, then slapped his hand against his head. "Hell! I didn't get the Salesman a birthday present!"

"He won't mind," Troy said. "Tell him you forgot."

"You don't think he'll be upset?"

"It's OK, Turner. Invite him out for lunch another time. He'll like that."

Turner smiled. "Good idea."

"Good luck," Alex said.

Turner got up and left. As he walked away, Alex noticed a man in a bright Hawaiian shirt and white trousers coming from the opposite direction. It was impossible to see the man's face because he was wearing sunglasses and a straw hat. But he must have been involved in some sort of terrible accident – his legs were dragging awkwardly and there seemed to be no life in his arms. For a moment he was right next to Turner on the boardwalk. Turner didn't notice him. Then, moving surprisingly quickly, he had gone.

Alex and Troy watched as Turner walked all the way along to *Mayfair Lady*. There was a ramp at the end of the jetty, leading up to deck level. It allowed the crew to wheel supplies on board. A couple of men were just finishing as Turner arrived. He spoke to them. One of them pointed in the direction of the saloon cabin. Turner went up the ramp and disappeared on board.

"What happens now?" Alex asked.

"We wait."

For about fifteen minutes nothing happened. Alex tried to talk to Troy but her attention was fixed on the boat and she said nothing. He wondered about the relationship between the two agents. They obviously knew each other well and Byrne had told him they'd worked together before. Neither of them showed their emotions, but he wondered if their friendship might be more than professional.

Then Alex saw Troy sit up in her seat. He followed her eyes back to the boat. Smoke was coming out of the funnel. The engines had started up. The two crewmen Turner had spoken to were on the jetty. One of them untied the boat, then climbed onboard. The other one walked off. Slowly, *Mayfair Lady* began to move away from her mooring.

"Something's gone wrong," Troy whispered. She wasn't talking to Alex. She was talking to herself.

"What d'you mean?"

Her head snapped round as she remembered he was there. "It was a ten minute meeting. Tom wasn't meant to be going anywhere."

Tom. It was the first time she had used his first name.

"Maybe he changed his mind," Alex suggested. "Maybe the Salesman invited him on a cruise."

"He wouldn't have gone. Not without me. Not

without cover. It's against company procedure."

"Then..."

"His cover's been blown." Troy's face was suddenly pale. "They must have found out he's an agent. They're taking him out to sea with them..."

She was standing up now but not moving, paralysed with indecision. The boat was still moving gracefully. Already a full half of its length was projecting out beyond the jetty. Even if she ran forward, she would never reach it in time.

"What are you going to do?" Alex asked.

"I don't know."

"Are they going to...?"

"If they know who he is, they'll kill him." She snapped the words as if this was somehow Alex's fault, as if it was a stupid question that he should never have asked. And maybe it was this that decided him. Suddenly, before he even knew what he was doing, he was on his feet and running. He was angry. He was going to show them that he was more than the dumb English kid they obviously thought he was.

"Alex!" Troy called out.

He ignored her. He had already reached the boardwalk. The two teenagers he had seen earlier were sitting in the sun, finishing their drinks, and they didn't see him snatch one of their skateboards and jump onto it. It was only as he pushed off, propelling himself over the wooden surface towards the departing boat, that one of them shouted in his direction, but by then it was too late.

Alex was balanced perfectly. Snowboards, skateboards, surfboards, they were all the same to him. And this skateboard was a beauty, a Flexdex downhill racer with ABEC5 racing bearings and kryptonic wheels. How typical of Miami kids to buy only the best. He shifted his weight, suddenly aware that he had neither helmet nor knee-pads. If he came off now, it was going to hurt. But that was the least of his worries. The boat was pulling away. Even as Alex watched, the stern with its churning propellers slid past the end of the jetty. Now the boat was at sea. He could see the name, *Mayfair Lady*, dwindling as it moved into the distance. In seconds it would be too far away to reach.

Alex hit the ramp that the men had been using to load and unload the boat. He soared upwards and suddenly he was in mid-air, flying. He felt the skateboard fall away from his feet, heard it splash into the sea. But his own momentum carried him forward. He wasn't going to make it!

The boat was moving too fast. Alex was plunging down now, following an arc that was going to miss the stern by centimetres. It would bring him crashing down into the water – and then what? The propellers! They would slice him to pieces. Alex stretched out his arms and somehow his scrabbling fingers made contact with the rail that curved round the back of the boat. His body smashed into the metal stern, his feet dipping into the water above the propellers.

He felt the breath punched out of him. Somebody on the boat must have heard. But he couldn't worry about that now. He would just have to hope that the noise of the engines had covered the collision. Using all his strength, he pulled himself up and over the rail. And then, finally, he was on the deck, soaked to the knees, his entire body aching from the impact. But he was onboard. And miraculously, he hadn't been seen.

He crouched down, taking stock of his surroundings. The stern deck was a small, semi-enclosed area, shaped like a horseshoe. In front of him was the saloon cabin with a single window facing back and the door a little further down the side. There was a stack of supplies underneath a tarpaulin and also two large cans. Alex unscrewed one of the lids and sniffed. It was full of petrol. The Salesman obviously planned to be away for some time.

The entire deck, both port and starboard, was overshadowed by a canopy hanging down on either side of the main saloon and there was a wooden lifeboat suspended on two pulleys above his head. Resting briefly against the stern rail, Alex knew he was safe provided nobody actually walked to the back of the boat. How many crew members would there be? Presumably there was a captain at the wheel. He might have someone with him. Looking up, Alex glimpsed a pair of feet crossing the upper deck on the roof of the saloon. That made three. There could be two or three more inside. Six perhaps in total?

He looked back. The port of Miami was already slipping away behind him. Alex got up and slipped off his shoes and socks. Then he crept forward, moving absolutely silently, still nervous about being spotted from the upper deck. The first two windows of the saloon were closed but the third was open and crouching below it he heard a voice. A man was talking. He had a thick Mexican accent and every time he spoke the letter S, he whistled softly.

"You are a foolish man. Your name is Tom

Turner. You work for the CIA. And I am going to kill you."

Another man spoke briefly. "You're wrong. I don't know what you're talking about." Alex recognized Turner's voice. He glanced left and right. Then, with his shoulders against the cabin wall, he levered himself upwards until his head reached the level of the window and he could look in.

The saloon cabin was rectangular, with a wooden floor partially covered by a carpet that had been rolled back – presumably to avoid bloodstains. Unlike the boat, the furniture was modern, office-like. There wasn't a great deal of it. Turner was sitting in a chair with his hands behind his back. Alex could see that some sort of parcel tape had been used to tie his arms and legs. He had already been beaten. His fair hair was damp and blood trickled out of the corner of his mouth.

There were two men in the cabin with him. One was a deckhand in jeans and black T-shirt, his stomach bulging out over his belt. The other had to be the Salesman. He was a round-faced man with very black hair and a small moustache. He was wearing a three-piece white suit, immaculately tailored, and brightly polished leather shoes. The deckhand was holding a gun, a large, heavy automatic. The Salesman was sitting in a cane chair, holding a glass of red wine. He rolled it in front of his nose, enjoying the aroma, then sipped.

"What a delicious wine!" he muttered. "This is Chilean. A Cabernet Sauvignon grown on my own estate. You see, my friend, I am successful. I have businesses all over the world. People want to drink wine? I sell wine. People want to take drugs? They are mad, but that is no concern of mine. I sell drugs. What is so wrong with that? I sell anything that anyone wishes to buy. But, you see, I am a careful man. I did not buy your story. I made certain enquiries. The Central Intelligence Agency is mentioned. And that is why you find yourself here."

"What do you want to know?" Turner rasped.

"I want to know when we are one hour out of Miami because that is when I intend to shoot you and dump you over the side." The Salesman smiled. "That is all."

Alex sank down again. There was no point listening to any more. He couldn't go into the cabin. There were two of them and only one of him. And although he had a weapon, it wouldn't be enough. Not against a gun. He needed a diversion.

Then he remembered the petrol. Glancing quickly at the upper deck he prepared to go back to the stern, then froze as the door of the bridge opened and a man came out. There was nothing Alex could do; nowhere he could hide. But he was lucky. The man, dressed in the faded uniform of a ship's captain, had been smoking a cigarette. He stopped long enough to throw the butt into the sea, then went back the way he had come without turning his head. It had been a close escape and Alex knew it could only be a matter of time before he was noticed. He had to move fast.

He ran on tiptoe to the petrol cans. He tried tilting one of them but it was too heavy. He looked around for a rag, couldn't find one and so took off his shirt, ripping it apart in his hands. Quickly he pushed the sleeve into the can, soaking it in petrol. Then he pulled it out, leaving only the end still dangling inside; a makeshift fuse. What would happen when he set fire to the petrol? Alex guessed that the explosion would be enough to attract the attention of everyone onboard but not strong enough to kill anyone or sink the boat. Since he was still going to be onboard, he would just have to hope he was right.

He reached into his pocket and took out the book of matches that he had been playing with in the restaurant. Cupping his hand to protect the flame from the breeze, he lit first one match, then the whole book. He touched the flame against the rag that had once been his shirt. The whole thing was alight in a second.

Running forward again, he returned to the saloon cabin. He could hear the Salesman still speaking inside.

"Another glass, I think. Yes. But then I'm afraid I must leave you. I have work to do."

Alex looked in. The Salesman was standing at a table, pouring himself a second glass of wine. Alex looked back over his shoulder. There was no one there. Nothing had happened. Why hadn't the petrol caught fire? Had the wind blown out his makeshift fuse?

And then it exploded. A great mushroom of flame and black smoke leapt into the air at the back of the boat, snatched away instantly by the wind. Somebody shouted. Alex saw that the petrol had splashed all over both decks. There was fire everywhere. The canopy right above his head was alight. Whatever had been packed underneath the tarpaulin was also blazing. More shouting. Footsteps thudded towards the stern deck. Now was the time to move.

"See what is happening!"

Alex heard the Salesman snap the command and a second later the deckhand came racing out. He disappeared round the other side of the cabin.

That just left the Salesman himself, on his own with Turner. Alex waited a few seconds, then stepped into the doorway, once again reaching into his trouser pocket. Turner saw him before the Salesman. His eyes widened. The Salesman turned. Alex saw that he had put down his glass and picked up a gun. For a moment neither of them moved. The Salesman was looking at a fourteen-year-old boy, barefoot and naked from the waist up. It obviously hadn't occurred to him that Alex could be any threat to him, that it was this boy who had set fire to his boat. And in that moment of hesitation, Alex made his move.

When he brought his hand up, he was holding a mobile phone. He had already dialled two nines before he'd gone in. He pressed the button for a third time as he aimed with the phone.

"It's for you!" he said.

He felt the phone shudder in his hand and, silently, the aerial spat out of the top, the plastic peeling back to reveal a shining needle. It travelled across the cabin and hit the Salesman square in the chest. The Salesman had reacted fast, already bringing his gun round. But a second later his eyes rolled and he slumped to the floor. Alex jumped over him, picked up a knife from the table and went over to Turner.

"What the hell...?" the CIA man began. Alex could see at once that he wasn't badly hurt. At the same time, his mood didn't seem to have improved. He looked from the phone to the unconscious figure of the Salesman. "What did you do to him?" he asked.

"He got the wrong number," Alex said. He cut through the adhesive tape.

Turner got to his feet and snatched up the gun that the Salesman had dropped. He checked the clip. The gun was fully loaded. "What happened?" he demanded. "I heard an explosion!"

"Yeah. That was me. I set the boat alight."

"What?"

"I set fire to the boat."

"But we're *on* the boat!"

"I know."

Before Alex could say any more, Turner moved, twisting round, snapping into combat position, arms up, legs apart. There was a stairwell at the far end of the cabin. Alex hadn't noticed it before. A figure had appeared, coming up from below. Turner fired twice. The figure crumpled back down. Turner stopped. Black smoke was seeping into the cabin. There was a second explosion and the entire boat rocked as if seized by a sudden squall. There was shouting outside on the deck. Looking out of the window, Alex could see flames.

"That must have been the second petrol tank," he said.

"How many tanks are there?"

"Just the two."

Turner seemed almost dazed. He forced himself to a decision. "The sea..." he said. "We're going to have to swim."

The CIA agent went first, edging sideways out of the cabin. Suddenly the deck was full of people. There were at least seven of them. Alex wondered where they had all come from. Two of them, young men in dirty white shirts and jeans, were fighting the flames with extinguishers. There were two on the roof, another on the deck. All of them were shouting.

Smoke was trailing into the sky behind the boat. The lifeboat was ablaze. Part of the canopy was on fire. At least nobody knew quite what had happened. Nobody had seen Alex come on board. The explosions had taken them all by surprise and all they cared about was getting the fire under control. However, as Turner came out of the cabin, one of the men on the upper deck saw him. He called out in Spanish.

"Move!" Turner shouted.

He ran for the edge of the boat. Alex followed.

There was the deafening chatter of a machine-gun and what was left of the canopy above his head was torn to shreds. Bullets smashed into the deck sending chips of wood flying. A glass bulb exploded. Alex wasn't even sure who was firing. All he knew was that he was trapped in the middle of smoke and flames and bullets and a lot of men who wanted him dead. He saw Turner dive over the side. There was another burst from the machine-gun and Alex felt the deck rip itself apart centimetres from his bare feet. He yelled out. Splinters slammed into his ankle and heels. He spurted forward and threw himself over the handrail. For what felt like an eternity everything was chaos. He could feel the wind racing over his bare shoulders. There were more gunshots. Then he plunged headfirst into the Atlantic and disappeared beneath the surface.

Alex allowed the ocean to embrace him. After the battlefield that *Mayfair Lady* had become, its water was warm and soothing. He swam down, a powerful breaststroke that took him ever deeper. Something whizzed past him and he realized that he was still being shot at. The further down he went, the safer he would be. He opened his eyes. The salt water stung but he needed to know how far he was going. He looked up. Light glimmered at the surface but there was no sign of the boat. His lungs were beginning to hurt. He needed to breathe. But still he waited. He would have been happy if he could have stayed underwater for an hour.

He couldn't. With his body crying out for oxygen, Alex kicked reluctantly for the surface. He came up gasping, with water streaming down his face. Turner was next to him. The CIA agent looked more dead than alive. Alex wondered if he had been hit, but there was no sign of any blood. Perhaps he was in shock.

"Are you all right?" Alex asked.

"Are you crazy?" Turner was so angry that he actually swallowed water as he spoke. He spluttered and fought to keep himself from going under. "You could have gotten us killed!"

"I just saved your life!" Alex was getting angry himself. He couldn't believe what he was hearing.

"You think so? Look!"

With a sense of dread, Alex swivelled round in the water. *Mayfair Lady* hadn't been destroyed. The fire was out. And the boat was coming back.

He had been underwater for perhaps ninety seconds. In that time, the ship had continued forward with all hands fighting the flames and nobody at the wheel. The engine had been at full throttle and it was now about five hundred metres away. But the captain had obviously returned to the bridge. The boat was wheeling round. Alex could make out four or five men standing at the bow. All of them were armed. They had seen him. One of them pointed and shouted. He and Turner were helpless, floating in the water with perhaps one weapon between them. Soon the boat would reach them. They were sitting targets, to be picked off like ducks in a fair.

What could he do? He looked at Turner, hoping the older man would produce something, some rabbit out of the hat. Didn't the CIA have gadgets? Where was the inflatable speedboat or the concealed aqualung? But Turner was helpless. He'd even managed to lose the gun.

Mayfair Lady completed her turn.

Turner swore.

The boat drew closer, slicing through the water.

And then it exploded. This time the explosions were huge, final. There were three of them, simultaneous, in the bow, the middle and the stern. *Mayfair Lady* was blown into three quite separate pieces, the funnel and main saloon heaving themselves out of the ocean as if trying to escape from the rest of the boat. Alex felt the shockwave travel through the water. The blast was deafening. A fist of water smashed into him, almost knocking him out. Pieces of wood, some of them on fire, rained down all around. He knew at once that nobody could have survived. And with that knowledge came a terrible thought.

Was it his fault? Had he killed them all?

Turner must have been thinking the same thing. He said nothing. The two of them watched as the three sections of what had once been a classic motor yacht sank and disappeared.

There was the sound of an outboard motor. Alex twisted round. A speedboat was racing towards them. He saw Belinda Troy at the wheel. She must have somehow commandeered it and come after them. She was on her own.

She helped Turner out of the water first, then Alex. For the first time, Alex realized that he couldn't see land. He felt that it had all happened so quickly. And yet *Mayfair Lady* had managed to put several kilometres between itself and the coast before it was destroyed.

"What happened?" Troy asked. The wind had caught her long hair and spread it all around her. She looked as if she was having hysterics. "I saw the boat blow. I thought you were—" She stopped and caught her breath. "What happened?" she repeated.

"It was the kid." Turner's voice was neutral. He was still trying to catch up with the events of the last few minutes. "He cut me free..."

"You were tied up?"

"Yes. The Salesman knew I was with the agency. He was going to kill me. Alex knocked him out. He had some sort of cell phone..." He was stating the facts, but there was no gratitude. The boat rocked gently. Nobody moved. "He blew up the boat. He killed them all."

"No." Alex shook his head. "The fire was out. You saw. They'd got the boat under control. They were turning round, about to come back—"

"For God's sake!" The CIA man was almost too tired to argue. "What do you think happened? You think one of the lights fused and *Mayfair Lady* just happened to blow up? You did it, Alex. You set the gas alight and that's what happened."

Gas. The American for petrol. It was one of the words they had tested him on at the Snackyard that morning. A century ago.

"I saved your life," Alex said.

"Yeah. Thanks, Alex." But Turner's voice was bleak.

Troy climbed behind the wheel and started the engine. The speedboat turned and they headed back towards the shore.

PASSPORT CONTROL

Alex had a window seat near the front of the plane. Troy was next to him with Turner on her other side, next to the aisle. A family on holiday (on *vacation*, he reminded himself). Troy was reading a magazine. Turner had a film script. He was meant to be a producer and had spent the journey making notes in the margin, just in case anyone happened to be looking. Alex was playing with a Game Boy Advance. He wondered about that. Turner had given it to him just before they'd left Miami. It had been very casual, standing in the departure lounge.

"Here, Alex. Something to keep you busy on the plane."

Alex was suspicious. He remembered that the last time he'd held a Game Boy, it had been filled with gadgets invented by Smithers at MI6. But as far as he could tell, this one was completely ordinary. At least, he'd got to level five of Rayman and so far it hadn't exploded in his hands.

He looked out the window. They had been in the air for about an hour. This had been their second flight of the day. They had gone from Miami to Kingston, Jamaica, and had caught the second plane there. They had been given the sort of snack that people expect, but never enjoy, on a plane. A sandwich, a small square of cake and a plastic tub of water. Now the stewardesses returned, hastily collecting the trays.

"This is your captain speaking. Please fasten your seat-belts and return your seats to the upright position. We will shortly be coming in to land."

Alex looked out of the window again. The sea was an extraordinary shade of turquoise. It didn't look like water at all. Then the plane dipped and suddenly he saw the island. Both islands. Cuba itself was to the north. Cayo Esqueleto was below it. There wasn't a cloud in the sky and for a moment the land mass was perfectly clear, laid out as if on the surface of the world, two patches of emerald green with a coastline that seemed to shimmer an electric blue. The plane tilted.

The islands disappeared and the next time Alex saw them the plane was coming in low, rushing towards a runway that seemed almost unreachable, hemmed in by offices and hotels and roads and palm trees. There was a control tower, ugly and misshapen. A low-rise terminal, prefabricated concrete and glass. Two more planes, already on the ground, surrounded by service trucks. There was a jolt as the back wheels came into contact with the tarmac. They were down.

Alex unclipped his seat-belt.

"Wait a minute, Alex," Troy said. "The seat-belt light is still on."

She was behaving like a mother. But the sort of mother she had chosen to be was bossy and demanding. Alex had to admit that it suited her. Anybody watching them might believe they were a family, but would have to add that they were an unhappy one. Since the events in Miami, the two agents had practically ignored him. Alex found it hard to work them out. Turner would be dead if it hadn't been for him, but neither of them would admit it – as if, in some way, he had dented their professional pride. And they still insisted that he had blown up *Mayfair Lady*, killing everyone onboard. Even Alex was finding it hard to avoid a sense of responsibility. It was true that he had set fire to the petrol. What other reason could there have been for the explosion that had followed?

He tried to put it out of his mind. The plane had come to a halt and everyone had stood up, fighting for the overhead lockers in the cramped compartment. As Alex reached up to take his own bag, the Game Boy almost fell out of his grip. Turner's head snapped round. Alex saw a flash of alarm in his eyes. "Be careful with that!" he said.

So he was right. There was something hidden inside the Game Boy. It was typical of the CIA agents to keep him in the dark. But that hadn't stopped them asking him to carry it in.

It was midday, the worst time to arrive. As they came out of the plane, Alex felt the heat reflecting off the tarmac. It was hard to breathe. The air was heavy and smelled of diesel. He was sweating before he had even reached the bottom of the steps and the arrivals lounge offered no relief. The air-conditioning had broken down and Alex soon found himself trapped in a confined space with two or three hundred people and no windows. The terminal was more like a large shed than a modern airport building. The walls were a drab olive green, decorated by posters of the island that looked twenty years out of date.

The passengers from Alex's flight caught up with passengers still being processed from the flight before and the result was a large, shapeless crowd of people and hand luggage, shuffling slowly forward towards three uniformed immigration officials in glass cabins. There were no queues. As each passport was stamped and one more person was allowed in, the crowd simply pressed forward, oozing through the security controls.

An hour later, Alex was still there. He was dirty and crumpled and he had a raging thirst. He looked to one side where a couple of old, splintered doors led into men's and women's toilets. There might be a tap inside but would the water even be drinkable? A guard in a brown shirt and trousers stood watching, leaning against the wall beside a floor-to-ceiling mirror, a machine-gun cradled in his arms. Alex wanted to stretch his arms but he was too hemmed in. There was an old woman with grey hair and a sagging face standing right next to him. She smelled of cheap perfume. As he half-turned, he found himself almost embraced by her and recoiled, unable to hide his disgust. He glanced up and saw that there was a single security camera set in the ceiling. He remembered how worried Joe Byrne had been about security at Santiago Airport. But it seemed to him that just about anyone could have walked in and nobody would have noticed. The guard looked bored and half asleep. The camera was probably out of focus.

At last they reached passport control. The official behind the glass screen was young, with black greasy hair and glasses. Turner slid three passports and three completed immigration forms through. The official opened them.

"Don't fidget, Alex," Troy said. "We'll be through in a minute."

"Sure, Mom."

The passport man looked up at them. His eyes showed no welcome at all. "Mr Gardiner? What is the purpose of your visit?" he demanded.

"Vacation," Turner replied.

The man's eyes flickered briefly over the passports and then at the people to whom they belonged. He slid them under a scanner, yawning at the same time. The guard that Alex had noticed was nowhere near. He was gazing out of the window, watching the planes.

"Where do you live?" the official asked.

"Los Angeles." Turner's face was blank. "I'm in the movie business."

"And your wife?"

"I don't work," Troy said.

The official had come to Alex's passport. He opened it and checked the picture against the boy who stood in front of him. "Alex Gardiner," he said.

"How you doing?" Alex smiled at him.

"This is your first trip to Cayo Esqueleto?"

"Yeah. But I hope it won't be my last."

The passport official stared at him, his eyes magnified by the glasses. He seemed completely uninterested. "What hotel are you staying at?" he asked.

"The Valencia," Turner said quietly. He had already written the name on the three immigration forms.

Another pause. Then the official picked up a stamp and brought it crashing down three times – three gunshots in the confined space of the kiosk. He handed back the passports. "Enjoy your visit to Cayo Esqueleto."

Alex and the two CIA agents passed through the immigration room and into the luggage hall where their cases were already waiting, circling endlessly on an old, creaking conveyor belt. And that was it, Alex thought. It couldn't have been easier! All that fuss and he hadn't even been needed in the first place.

He picked up his case.

At the same time, although he was unaware of it, his picture and passport details were already being transmitted to police headquarters in Havana, Cuba, along with those of Turner and Troy. The "family" had actually been photographed three times. Once by the overhead camera that Alex had seen in the arrivals lounge, but which was far more sophisticated than he would have believed. As old-fashioned as it looked, it could zoom in on the hole in a man's button or a single word written in a diary and blow it up fifty times if needed. They had been photographed a second time by a camera behind the mirror next to the toilets. And finally, a profile close-up shot had been taken by a camera concealed in a brooch worn by an old lady who smelled of cheap perfume and who had not, in fact, arrived on a plane but who was always there, mingling with the new arrivals, moving in on anyone who had aroused the suspicions of the people she worked for. The immigration forms that Turner had filled in were also on their way, sealed in a plastic bag. His answers to the standard questions mattered less to the authorities than the forms themselves. The paper had been specially formulated to record fingerprints, and in less than an hour these would be digitally scanned and checked against a huge database in the same police building.

The invisible machine that operated in the airport at Santiago had been focused on Turner and Troy before they had even arrived. They were American. They had said they were on vacation and their luggage (which had, of course, been searched as it came off the plane) contained the sunscreen, beach towels and basic medicines that you would expect an ordinary American family to pack. The labels on their clothes showed that they had all been bought in Los Angeles. But a single receipt tucked into the top pocket of one of Turner's shirts told another story. He had recently bought a book from a shop in Langley, Virginia. Langley is where the headquarters of the CIA are based. The little scrap of paper had been enough to set alarm bells ringing. This was the result.

The officer in charge of security at the airport was watching them carefully. He was sitting in a small, windowless office and their images were right in front of him, on a bank of television screens. He watched them as they continued out of baggage reclaim and into the arrivals hall. His finger hovered briefly beside a red button on his console. It still wasn't too late. He could pull them back in before they had reached the taxi stand. There were plenty of cells buried deep in the basement. And when normal questioning failed, there were always drugs.

And yet...

The head of security was called Rodriguez and he was good at his job. He had interrogated so many American spies that he sometimes said he could recognize one at a hundred metres. He had spotted "Mr and Mrs Gardiner" before they had even crossed the runway and had sent out his deputy to take a closer look. This was the bored-looking guard that Alex had seen.

But this time Rodriguez wasn't sure – and he couldn't afford to make mistakes. After all, Cayo Esqueleto needed its tourists. It needed the money that tourism brought. He might have his suspicions about the two adults, but they were two adults travelling with a child. He had over-heard the brief conversation between Alex and the passport official. There were microphones concealed throughout the immigration hall. How old was the boy? Fourteen? Fifteen? Just another American kid being given two weeks on the beach.

Rodriguez made up his mind. He lifted his hand

away from the alarm button. It was better to avoid the bad publicity. He watched the family disappear into the crowd.

Even so, the authorities would keep an eye on them. Later that day, just to be on the safe side, he would compile a report which would be sent along with the photographs and fingerprints to the local police in Cayo Esqueleto. A copy would also be forwarded to the very important gentleman who lived in the Casa de Oro. And perhaps someone would be sent to the Hotel Valencia to keep a close eye on the new arrivals.

Rodriguez settled in his chair and lit a cigarette. Another plane had landed. He leaned forward and began to examine the arriving crowd.

The Valencia was one of those amazing hotels that Alex usually saw in dream holiday prizes on game shows. It was tucked away in a crescent-shaped cove with miniature villas spread out along the beach and a low-rise reception area almost lost in a miniature jungle of exotic shrubs and flowers. There was a doughnut-shaped swimming pool with a bar in the inner ring and stools poking up just above the level of the water. The whole place seemed to be asleep. This was certainly true of the few guests Alex could see, lying motionless on sun-loungers.

Alex and his "parents" were sharing a villa with two bedrooms and a veranda sheltered from the sun by a sloping straw roof. There was a clump of palm trees, white sand, then the impossible blue of the Caribbean. Alex sat down briefly on his bed. It was covered with a single white sheet and a fan turned slowly in the ceiling. A brilliant green and yellow bird perched briefly on his windowsill then flew off towards the sea as if inviting him.

"Can I go for a swim?" he asked. He wouldn't normally have asked their permission but he figured it probably suited his role.

"Sure, honey!" Troy was unpacking. She had already warned Alex that he would have to stay in character whenever they were in the villa. The hotel might well be bugged. "But you be careful!"

Alex changed into his shorts and ran across the sand into the sea.

The water was perfect; warm and crystal clear. There was no shingle, only the softest carpet of sand. Tiny fish swam all around him, scattering instantly when he stretched out his hand. For the first time in his life, Alex was glad he had met Alan Blunt. This was certainly better than hanging out in west London. For once, things seemed to be going his way.

After he had swum, he climbed into a hammock stretched out between two trees and relaxed. It was about half past four and the afternoon felt as hot as it had been when they arrived. A waiter came up to him and he asked for a lemonade, charging it to his villa. His mum and dad could pay.

Mum and dad.

As he swung gently from side to side with the water trickling through his hair and drying on his chest, Alex wondered what his real parents would have been like if they hadn't both died in a plane crash soon after he was born. And what would it have been like for him, growing up in an ordinary home, with a mother to run to when he was hurt and a father to play with, to borrow money from or sometimes to avoid? Would it have made him any different? He would have been an ordinary schoolboy, worrying about exams – not spies and salesmen and exploding boats. He might have been a softer person. He'd probably have had more friends. And he certainly wouldn't have been lying in a hammock in the grounds of the Hotel Valencia.

He stayed there until his hair was dry and he knew it was time to get out of the sun. Turner and Troy hadn't come out to find him and he suspected they were busy with their own affairs. He was still sure there were a lot of things they weren't telling him. He remembered the Game Boy Advance. They had only mentioned it at the very last minute, just as they were about to get onto the plane. Could it be that they had wanted him to carry it onto the island, knowing that a fourteen year old would have less chance of being searched?

Alex rolled out of the hammock and dropped down onto the sand. A local man was walking past, selling strings of beads to the tourists out on the beach. He glanced at Alex and held up a necklace; a dozen different shells on a leather cord. Alex shook his head, then walked the short distance back to his villa. He still had the Game Boy in his hand luggage. Turner had forgotten to ask for it back. Alex slipped quietly into his room, took it out and examined it again. There seemed to be nothing out of the ordinary. It was bright blue with the single game, Rayman, lodged in the back. Alex weighed it in his hands. As far as he could tell it wasn't any heavier or lighter than it should have been.

Then he remembered. The Game Boy he had once been given by MI6 had been activated by pressing the PLAY button three times. Perhaps this model would work the same way. Alex turned it over and pressed the button. Once, twice ... a third time. Nothing happened. He gazed for a moment at the blank screen, annoyed with himself. He was wrong. It was just a game, given to him to keep him quiet on the plane. It was time to get dressed. He put the Game Boy on the bedside table and stood up.

The Game Boy squawked.

Alex snapped round, recognizing the sound without yet knowing what it was. The Game Boy was still squawking, a strange, metallic rattling sound. The screen had suddenly come to life. It was pulsating, green and white. What did it mean? He picked the machine up again. At once the noise died away and the lights on the screen faded out. He moved the Game Boy back towards the bedside table. It burst back into life.

Alex looked at the bedside table. There was nothing on it apart from an old-fashioned alarm clock, supplied by the hotel. He opened the drawer. There was a bible inside with the text printed in Spanish and English. Nothing else. So what was causing the Game Boy to act in this way? He swung it away. It became silent. He moved it back to the table. It started again.

The clock...

Alex looked more closely at the dial. The clock had a luminous face. He pressed the Game Boy right up against the glass and the squawking was suddenly louder than ever. Now Alex understood. The numbers on the clock face were faintly radioactive. That was what the Game Boy was picking up.

The Game Boy concealed a Geiger counter. Alex smiled grimly. Rayman was certainly the right game for this machine. Except that the rays it was looking for were radioactive ones.

What did it mean? Turner and Troy weren't on the island for a simple surveillance operation. He had been right. Both Blunt in London and Byrne in Miami had been lying to him from the very start. Alex knew that he was sitting only a few kilometres south of Cuba. Something he had learned in history came to his mind. Cuba. The nineteen-sixties. The Cuban missile crisis. Nuclear weapons trained on America...

He still couldn't be certain. He might be jumping to conclusions. But the fact was that the CIA had smuggled a Geiger counter into Skeleton Key and, as crazy as it sounded, there could only be one reason why they needed it.

They were looking for a nuclear bomb.

BROTHERHOOD SQUARE

Alex said little at dinner that night. Although the hotel had seemed empty earlier in the day, he was surprised how many guests had appeared for dinner in their loose skirts, shirts and suntans, and he knew it would be impossible to talk openly now.

They were sitting on the restaurant terrace which overlooked the sea, eating fish – as fresh as Alex had ever tasted – served with rice, salad and black beans. After the intense heat of the afternoon, the air was cool and welcoming. Two guitarists, lit by candles, were playing soft Latin music. Cicadas rasped and rattled in their thousands, hidden in the undergrowth.

The three of them talked like any family would. The towns they were going to visit, the beaches where they wanted to swim. Turner told a joke and Troy laughed loud enough to turn heads. But it was all fake. They weren't going anywhere and the joke hadn't been funny. Despite the food and the surroundings, Alex found himself hating every minute of the role he had been forced to play. The last time he had sat down with a family had been with Sabina and her parents in Cornwall. It seemed a very long time ago and this meal, with these people, somehow turned the memory sour.

But at last it was over and Alex was able to excuse himself and go to bed. He went back to his room, swinging the door shut behind him. For a moment he stood there with his shoulders resting against the wood. He looked around him. Something was wrong. He stepped forward carefully, his nerves jangling. Someone had been there. His case, which had been closed when he left, was now open. Had someone from the hotel been in and searched the room while he was at dinner? Were they still there now? He looked in the bathroom and behind the curtains. No one. Then he went over to the case. It took him a few moments to realize that only the Game Boy was missing. So that was what had happened! Turner or Troy must have somehow slipped into the room while he was out. The Game Boy with its hidden Geiger counter was central to their mission. They had taken it back.

Alex undressed quickly and got into bed, but suddenly he wasn't tired. He lay in the darkness, listening to the waves breaking against the sand. He could see thousands of stars through the open window. He had never realized there were so many of them, nor that they could shine so bright. Turner and Troy returned to their room about half an hour later. He heard them talking in low voices but couldn't make out what they said. He pulled the sheet over his head and forced himself to sleep.

The first thing he saw when he woke up the next morning was a note pushed under his door. He got out of bed and picked it up. It was written in block capitals.

GONE FOR A WALK. THOUGHT YOU NEEDED A REST. WE'LL CATCH UP WITH YOU LATER. MOM XXX.

Alex tore the note in half – and then in half again. He scattered the pieces in the wastepaper basket and went out to breakfast. It occurred to him that it was a strange set of parents who would walk off, leaving their son behind, but he supposed there were probably plenty of families, with nannies and au pairs, who often did the same. He spent the morning on the beach, reading. There were some other boys of about his own age playing in the sea and he thought of joining them. But they didn't speak English and seemed too self-contained. At eleven o'clock, his "parents" still hadn't returned. Suddenly Alex was fed up, sitting there on his own in the grounds of the hotel. He was on an island on the other side of the world. He might as well see some of it! He got dressed and set off into town.

The heat struck him the moment he stepped outside the grounds of the hotel. The road curved inland, away from the sea, following a line of scrubland on one side and what looked like a tobacco plantation – a mass of fat, green leaves rising to chest height – on the other. The landscape was flat but there was no breeze coming in from the sea. The air was heavy and still. Alex was soon sweating and had to swat at the flies that seemed determined to follow him every step of the way. A few buildings, sun-bleached wood and corrugated iron, sprang up around him. A fly buzzed in his ear. He beat it away.

It took him twenty minutes to reach Puerto

Madre, a fishing village that had grown into a dense and cluttered town. The buildings were an amazing jumble of different styles; rickety wooden shops, marble and brick houses, huge stone churches. Everything had been beaten down and baked by the sun – and sunlight was everywhere; in the dust, in the vivid colours, in the smells of spice and overripe fruit.

The noise was deafening. Radio music – jazz and salsa – blasted out of open windows. Extraordinary American cars, vintage Chevrolets and Studebakers like brilliantly coloured toys, jammed the streets, their horns blaring as they tried to make their way past horses and carts, motorized rickshaws, cigarette sellers and shoeshine boys. Old men in vests sat outside the cafés blinking in the sunlight. Women in tight-fitting dresses stood languidly in the doorways. Alex had never been anywhere louder or dirtier or more alive.

Somehow he found himself in the main square with a great statue at the centre; a revolutionary soldier with a rifle at his side and a grenade hanging from his belt. There must have been at least a hundred market stalls jammed into the square, selling fruit and vegetables, coffee beans, souvenirs, old books and T-shirts. And everywhere there were crowds, strolling in and out of the dollar shops and the ice-cream parlours, sitting at tables beneath sweeping colonnades, queuing up in the fast food restaurants and the *paladares* – tiny restaurants located inside private houses.

There was a street sign bolted to a wall. It read: PLAZA DE FRATERNIDAD. Alex had enough Spanish to translate that. Brotherhood Square. He somehow doubted that he would find much brotherhood here. A fat man in an old and dirty linen suit suddenly lurched up to him.

"You want cigars? The best Havana cigars. But at cheap, cheap price."

"Hey, *amigo*. I sell you a T-shirt..."

"*Muchacho!* You bring your parents to my bar..."

Before he knew it, he was surrounded. Alex realized how much he must stand out in this crowd of dark, tropical people milling about in their brightly coloured shirts and straw hats. He was hot and thirsty. He looked around him for somewhere to get a drink.

And that was when he saw Turner and Troy. The two special agents were sitting at a wrought iron table in front of one of the smarter restaurants, shaded by a great vine that sprawled and tumbled over the pockmarked wall. A neon sign hung over them, advertising Montecristo cigars. They were with a man, an islander, obviously deep in conversation. All three of them had drinks. Alex moved towards them, wondering if it would be possible to hear what they were saying.

The man they were talking to looked about seventy years old and was dressed in a dark shirt, loose trousers and a beret. He was smoking a cigarette which seemed to have been pushed through his lips dragging the skin with it. His face, arms and neck were sun-beaten and withered. But as he drew closer, Alex saw the light and the strength in his eyes. Troy said something and the man laughed, picked up his glass with a hand that was all bone and threw back the contents in one. He wiped the back of his hand across his mouth, said something and walked away. Alex had arrived just too late to eavesdrop on the conversation. He decided to make himself known.

"Alex!" As ever, Troy didn't look glad to see him.

"Hi, Mom." Alex sat down without being invited. "Any chance of a drink?"

"What are you doing here?" Turner asked. Once again his mouth was a straight line. His eyes were empty. "We told you to stay at the hotel."

"I thought this was meant to be a family holiday," Alex said. "And anyway, I finished searching the hotel this morning. There aren't any nuclear weapons there, in case you were wondering..."

Turner stared. Troy looked around nervously. "Keep your voice down!" she snapped, as if anyone could hear him in the din of the square.

"You lied to me," Alex said. "Whatever the reason you're here, you're not just spying on General Sarov. Why don't you tell me what this is really about?"

There was a long silence.

"What do you want to drink?" Troy asked.

Alex glanced down at Troy's glass. It contained a pale yellow liquid that looked good. "What have you got?" he asked.

"A *mojito*. It's a local speciality. A mixture of rum, fresh lemon juice, crushed ice, soda and mint leaves."

"That sounds fine. I'll have the same. Without the rum."

Turner called a waiter over and spoke briefly in Spanish. The waiter nodded and hurried away.

Meanwhile, Troy had come to a decision. "All right, Alex," she said. "We'll tell you what you want to know—"

"That's against orders!" Turner interrupted.

Troy looked angrily at him. "What choice do we have? Alex obviously knows about the Game Boy."

"The Geiger counter," Alex said.

Troy nodded. "Yes, Alex, that's what it is. And it's the reason why we're here." She lifted her own drink and took a sip. "We didn't want you to know this because we didn't want to frighten you."

"That's very kind of you."

"We were ordered not to!" She scowled. "But ... all right, since you know so much, you might as well know the rest of it. We believe there's a nuclear device hidden on this island."

"General Sarov...? You think he's got a nuclear bomb?"

"We shouldn't be doing this," Turner muttered.

But this time Troy ignored him. "Something is happening, here, on Skeleton Key," she went on. "We don't know what it is, but if you want the truth, it actually frightens us. In a few days' time, Boris Kiriyenko, the Russian president, is arriving for a two-week vacation. That's not such a big deal. He knew Sarov a long time ago. They were kids together. And it's not as if the Russians are our enemies any more."

Alex knew all this already. It was what Blunt

had told him in London.

"But recently, and quite by coincidence, Sarov came to our attention. Turner and I were investigating the Salesman. And we discovered that among all the other things he'd been selling, he'd managed to get his hands on a kilogram of weapons grade uranium, smuggled out of Eastern Europe. For what it's worth, this is one of the biggest nightmares facing the security services today – the sale of uranium. But he'd done it – and if that wasn't bad enough, the person he'd sold it to—"

"—was Sarov." Alex finished the sentence.

"Yes. A plane flew into Skeleton Key and it didn't fly out again. Sarov was there to meet it." She paused. "And now, suddenly, we've got a meeting between these two men – the old general and the new president – and there may be a nuclear bomb in the picture. So you won't be surprised to hear that there are a whole lot of worried people in Washington. That's why we're here."

Alex absorbed what he was being told. Inside, he was seething. Blunt had promised him two weeks in the sun. But it looked like he'd been sent to the front line of World War Three.

"If it is a bomb, what's Sarov planning to do

with it?" Alex asked.

"If we knew that, we wouldn't be here!" she snapped. Alex looked at her closely. He was amazed to see that she really was scared. She was trying not to show it but it was there, in her eyes and the tautness of her jaw.

"Our job is to find the nuclear material," Turner said.

"With the Geiger counter."

"Yes. We need to break into Casa de Oro and take a look around. That's what we were talking about just now."

"Who was he? The man you were with?"

Turner sighed. He had already said much more than he wanted to "His name is Garcia. He's one of our assets."

"Assets?"

"That means he works for us," Troy explained. "We've been paying him over the years to keep us informed and to help us when we're here."

"He has a boat," Turner continued, "and we're going to need it because there's only one way into the Casa de Oro – and that's by sea. The house is built on a sort of plateau right at the tip of the island. It's an old sugar plantation. They used to grow sugar cane there and they've got an old mill that's still in full working order. Anyway, there's only one road that reaches it and it's narrow, with a steep drop down to the sea on both sides. There are security men and a gate. We'd never get in that way."

"But by boat—" Alex began.

"Not by boat..." Turner hesitated, wondering if he should go on. He looked at Troy, who nodded. "We're going to use scuba. You see, we know something that Sarov may not. There's a way into the grounds of the villa that goes past his defences. It's a natural fault line, a shaft inside the cliff that runs all the way from the top to the bottom."

"You're going to climb it?"

"There are metal rungs. Garcia's family has been on the island for centuries and they know every inch of the coastline. He swears the ladder is still there. Three hundred years ago it was used by smugglers to get from the villa to the beach without being seen. There was a cave at the bottom. The shaft – they call it the Devil's Chimney – runs all the way up and comes out somewhere in the garden. That's our way in."

"Wait a minute." Alex was confused. "You said you were going to use scuba."

Troy nodded. "The water level has risen all around the island and the entrance to the cave is now submerged. It's about twenty metres underwater. But that's great for us. Most people have forgotten the cave is even there at all. Certainly, it won't be guarded. We swim down in scuba gear. We climb the ladder and get into the grounds. We search the villa."

"And if you find the bomb?"

"That's not our problem, Alex. Our work will be done."

The waiter arrived with Alex's drink. He picked up the glass. Even the feel of it, cold against his skin, came as a relief. He drank some. It was sweet and surprisingly refreshing. He set the glass down.

"I want to come with you," he said.

"Forget it. No way!" Troy sounded incredulous. "Why do you think I've told you all this? Only because you know too much already and I need you to understand that we mean business. You have to keep out of the way. This is not a child's game. We're not zapping the bad guy on a computer screen! This is the real thing, Alex. And you're going to stay in the hotel and wait for us to get back!"

"I'm coming with you," Alex insisted. "Maybe you've forgotten, but this is meant to be a family holiday. You dump me on my own in the hotel a second time, maybe somebody's going to notice. Maybe they're going to start wondering where you are."

Turner fiddled with the collar of his shirt. Troy looked away.

"I won't get in your way," Alex sighed. "I'm not asking to come scuba-diving with you. Or climbing. I just want to be on the boat. Think about it. If the three of us go together, it'll look more like a family cruise."

Turner nodded slowly. "You know, Troy, the kid has a point."

Troy picked up her drink and gazed into it moodily, as if trying to find an answer inside the glass. "All right," she said at last. "You can come with us if that's what you really want. But you're not part of this, Alex. Your job was to help get us onto the island and if you ask me, we didn't even need you for that. You saw the security at the airport, it was a joke! But OK, since you're here, you might as well come along for the ride. But I don't want to hear you. I don't want to see you. I don't want to know you're there."

"Whatever you say," Alex sat back. He had got what he wanted, but he had to ask himself why he wanted it at all. Given the choice, he would have preferred to take the first plane off the island and put as much distance as possible between himself and the CIA and Sarov and the whole lot of them.

But that was a choice he didn't have. All Alex knew was that he didn't want to spend time in the hotel on his own, worrying. If there really was a bomb somewhere on the island, he wanted to be the first to hear about it. And there was something else. Turner and Troy seemed confident enough about this Devil's Chimney. They had assumed that it wasn't guarded and that it would take them all the way to the top. But they had been equally confident when they had gone to the Salesman's birthday party, and that had almost got Turner killed.

Alex finished his drink. "All right," he said. "So when do we go?"

Troy fell silent. Turner took out his wallet and paid for the drinks. "Straight away," he said. "We're doing it tonight."

THE DEVIL'S CHIMNEY

It was late afternoon when they set out from Puerto Madre, leaving the port with its fish markets and pleasure cruisers behind them. Turner and Troy were going to make the dive while it was still light. They would find the cave and wait there until sunset, then climb up into Casa de Oro under cover of darkness. That was the plan.

The man called Garcia had a boat that had known the sea too long. It wheezed and spluttered out of the harbour, trailing a cloud of evil-smelling black smoke. Rust had rippled and then burst through every surface like some bad skin disease. The boat had no visible name. A few flags fluttered from the mast, but they were little more than rags, with any trace of their original colours faded long ago. There were six air cylinders lashed to a bench underneath a canopy. They were the only new equipment in sight.

Garcia himself had greeted Alex with a mixture of hostility and suspicion. Then he had spoken at length, in Spanish, with Turner. Alex had spent the best part of a year in Barcelona with his uncle and understood enough of the language to follow what they were saying.

"You never talked about a boy. What do you think this is? A tourist excursion? Who is he? Why did you bring him here?"

"It's none of your business, Garcia. Let's go."

"You paid for two passengers." Garcia held up two withered fingers, every bone and sinew showing through. "Two passengers ... that was what we agreed."

"You're being paid well enough. There's no point arguing. The boy's coming and that's the end of it!"

After that, Garcia fell into sullen silence. Not that there would have been any point talking anyway. The noise of the engine was too great.

Alex watched as the coastline of Cayo Esqueleto slipped past. He had to admit that Blunt had been right – the island was strangely beautiful with its extraordinary, deep colours; the palm trees packed together, separated from the sea by a brilliant ribbon of white sand. The sun was hovering, a perfect circle, over the horizon. A brown pelican, clumsy and comical on the ground, shot out of a pine tree and soared gracefully over their heads. Alex felt strangely at peace. Even the noise of the engine seemed to have drifted away.

After about half an hour, the land began to rise up and he realized they had reached the north point of the island. The vegetation fell back and suddenly he was looking at a sheer rock wall that dropped all the way, without interruption, to the sea. This must be the isthmus that he had been told about, with the road leading to the Casa de Oro somewhere at the top. There was no sign of the house itself but, craning his neck, he could just make out the top of a tower, white and elegant, with a pointed red slate roof. A watchtower. There was a single figure framed in an archway, barely more than a speck. Somehow Alex knew that it was an armed guard.

Garcia turned off the engine and moved to the back of the boat. For such an old man, he seemed very agile. He picked up an anchor and threw it over the side, then hoisted a flag – this one more identifiable than the others. It showed a diagonal white stripe on a red background. Alex recognized the international scuba-diving sign.

Troy came over to him. "We'll go down here and swim in to the coast," she said.

Alex looked up at the figure in the tower. There was a glint of sunlight reflecting off something. A pair of binoculars? "I think we're being watched," he said.

Troy nodded. "Yes. But it doesn't matter. Dive boats aren't allowed to come here but they sometimes do. They're used to it. The shore is strictly off-limits but there's a wreck somewhere ... people swim to that. We'll be fine, provided we don't draw attention to ourselves. Just don't do anything stupid, Alex."

Even now she couldn't resist lecturing him. Alex wondered what he would have to do to impress these people. He said nothing.

Turner had taken off his shirt, showing a hairless, muscular chest. Alex watched as he stripped down to his trunks, then pulled on a wetsuit which he had taken from a small cabin below. Quickly the two CIA agents got ready, attaching air cylinders to their buoyancy jackets – BCDs – then adding weight belts, masks and snorkels. Garcia was smoking, sitting to one side and watching all this with quiet amusement, as if it really had nothing to do with him.

At last they were ready. Turner had brought a waterproof bag with him and he unzipped it. Alex noticed the Game Boy sealed in a plastic bag inside. There were also maps, torches, knives and a harpoon gun.

"Leave it all, Turner," Troy said.

"The Game Boy...?"

"We'll come back for it." Troy turned to Alex. "Right, Alex," she said. "Listen up! We're going to make an exploratory dive to begin with. We'll be gone about twenty minutes. No longer. We need to find the cave entrance and check there are no security devices in operation." She glanced at her watch. It was only half past six. "The sun won't set for another hour," she continued. "We don't want to spend that long sitting in the cave, so we'll come back to the boat for the rest of our equipment, change tanks and make a second journey back. You don't have to worry about anything. As far as the people in the villa are concerned, we're just tourists doing a sunset dive."

"I'm a qualified diver," Alex said.

"The hell with that!" Turner cut in.

Troy agreed. "You talked your way onto the boat," she said. "Fine. Personally, I wish you'd stayed in the hotel. But maybe you were right about that, it might have raised suspicions."

"You're not coming with us," Turner said. He looked at Alex coldly. "We don't want any more people killed. You stay here with Garcia and leave the rest to us."

The two agents made their all-important buddy checks, each one looking over the other's equipment. No pipes twisted. Air in the tanks. Weights and releases. Finally, they went over to the side of the boat and sat with their backs facing the sea. They both put on their fins. Turner gave Troy the all-clear sign: second finger and thumb forming an O, with the other fingers raised. They lowered their masks and rolled over backwards, disappearing immediately into the depths of the sea.

That was the last time Alex saw them alive.

He sat with Garcia on the gently rocking boat. The sun was almost touching the horizon and a few clouds, deep red, had intruded into the sky. The air was warm and pleasant. Garcia sucked on his cigarette and the tip glowed.

"You American?" he asked suddenly, speaking in English.

"No. I'm English."

"Why you here?" Garcia smiled as if amused to

find himself alone at sea with an English boy.

"I don't know." Alex shrugged. "How about you?"

"Money." The one word answer was enough.

Garcia came over and sat down next to Alex, examining him with two dark eyes that were suddenly very serious. "They don't like you," he said.

"I don't think so," Alex agreed.

"You know why?"

Alex said nothing.

"They are grown-ups. They think they are good at what they do. And then they find a child who is better. And not only that. He is an English child. Not an Americano!" Garcia chuckled and Alex wondered how much he had been told. "It makes them feel uncomfortable. It's the same all over the world."

"I didn't ask to be here," Alex said.

"But still you came. They would have been happier without you."

The boat creaked. A light breeze had sprung up, rippling the flags. The sun was sinking faster now and the whole sky was turning to blood. Alex looked at his watch. Ten to seven. The twenty minutes had passed quickly. He scanned the surface of the ocean but there was no sign of Turner or Troy.

Another five minutes passed. Alex was beginning to feel uneasy. He didn't know the two agents well, but guessed they were people who did everything by the book. They had their procedures, and if they said twenty minutes, they meant twenty minutes. They had been underwater now for twenty-five. Of course, they had enough oxygen for an hour. But even so, Alex wondered why they were taking so long.

A quarter of an hour later, they still hadn't come back. Alex couldn't disguise his fears. He was pacing the deck, looking left and right, searching for the tell-tale bubbles that would show them coming up, hoping to see their arms and heads breaking the surface of the water. Garcia hadn't moved. Alex wondered if the old man was even awake. A full forty minutes had passed since Turner and Troy had submerged.

"Something's wrong," Alex said. Garcia didn't answer. "What are we going to do?" Still Garcia refused to speak and Alex became angry. "Didn't they have a back-up plan? What did they tell you to do?"

"They tell me to wait for them." Garcia opened his eyes. "I wait an hour. I wait two hours. I wait all night..."

"But in another ten or fifteen minutes they're going to run out of air."

"Maybe they enter the Devil's Chimney. Maybe they climb up!"

"No. That wasn't their plan. And anyway, they've left all their equipment behind." Suddenly Alex had made up his mind. "Have you got any more scuba gear? Another BCD?"

Garcia stared at Alex, surprised. Then he slowly nodded.

Five minutes later, Alex stood on the deck dressed only in shorts and a T-shirt, with an oxygen cylinder strapped to his back and two respirators – one to breathe through, the other spare – dangling at his side. He would have liked to put on a wetsuit, but he hadn't been able to find one his size. He would just have to hope that the water wasn't too cold. The BCD he was wearing was old and it was too big for him, but he had quickly tested it and at least it worked. He looked at his instrument console; pressure gauge, depth gauge and compass. He had 3000psi in his air tank. More than he would need. Finally, he had a knife strapped to his leg. He probably wouldn't use it and would never normally have worn it. But he needed the reassurance. He went over to the side of the boat and sat down.

Garcia shook his head disapprovingly. Alex knew he was right. He was breaking the single most critical rule in the world of scuba-diving. Nobody ever dives alone. He had been taught scuba by his uncle when he was eleven years old and if Ian Rider had been here now he would have been speechless with anger and disbelief. If you get into trouble – a snagged air hose or a valve failure – and you don't have a buddy, you're dead. It's as simple as that. But this was an emergency. Turner and Troy had been gone for forty-five minutes. Alex had to help.

"You take this," Garcia said suddenly. He was holding an out of date dive computer. It would show Alex how deep he was and how long he had been down.

"Thanks," Alex said. He took it.

Alex pulled his mask down, pushed the mouthpiece between his lips and breathed in. He could feel the oxygen and nitrogen mix rushing into the back of his throat. It had a slightly stale taste but he could tell it wasn't contaminated. He crossed his hands, holding his mask and respirator in place, then rolled over backwards. He felt his arm knock against something on the side as the world spun upside down. The water rushed up to greet him and then his vision was pulled apart like a curtain opening as he found himself plunging into the water.

He had left enough air in the BCD to keep him afloat and he made one last check, getting his bearings on the coastline so that he would know where to swim to and, more importantly, how to get back. At least the sea was still warm, although Alex knew that, with the sun rapidly setting, it wouldn't be for long. Cold is a dangerous enemy for the scuba-diver, sapping the strength and concentration. The deeper he went, the colder it would get. He couldn't afford to hang around. He released the air from the BCD. At once the weights began to drag him down. The sea rose up and devoured him.

He swam down, squeezing his nose and blowing hard – equalizing – to stop the pain in his ears. For the first time he was able to look around him. There was still enough sunlight to illuminate the sea and Alex caught his breath, marvelling at the astonishing beauty of the underwater world. The water was dark blue and perfectly clear. There were a few coral heads dotted around him, the shapes and colours as alien as anything it's possible to find on the earth. He felt completely at peace, the sound of his own breathing echoing in his ears and each breath releasing a cascade of silver bubbles. With his arms loosely folded across his chest, Alex let his fins propel him towards the shore. He was fifteen metres down, about five metres above the sea bed. A family of brightly coloured groupers swam past him; fat lips, bulging eyes and strange, misshapen bodies. Hideous and beautiful at the same time. It had been a year since Alex had last gone diving and he wished he had time to enjoy this. He kicked forward. The groupers darted away, alarmed.

It didn't take him long to reach the edge of the cliff. The sea wall was of course much more than a wall; a seething mass of rock, coral, vegetation and fish life. A living thing. Huge gorgonian fans – leaves made of a thousand tiny bones – waved slowly from side to side. Clumps of coral exploded brilliantly all around him. A school of about a thousand tiny silver fish flickered past. There was a slither of movement as a moray eel disappeared behind a rock. He glanced at the dive computer. At least it seemed to be working. It told him he had been down for seven minutes.

He had to find the entrance to the cave. That was why he was here. He forced himself to ignore the colours and sights of the underwater kingdom and concentrate on the rock face. The time he had spent taking his bearings before the dive paid off now. He knew more or less where the tower at the Casa de Oro stood in relation to the boat and swam in that direction, keeping the rock wall on his left. Something long and dark flashed past high above him. Alex saw it out of the corner of his eye but by the time he had turned his head it was gone. Was there a boat on the surface? Alex went down another couple of metres, searching for the cave.

In the end, it wasn't hard to find. The entrance was circular, like a gaping mouth. This impression was heightened when Alex swam closer and looked inside. The cave hadn't always been underwater and over a period of time – millions of years – stalactites and stalagmites had grown, needle-sharp spears that hung down from the ceiling and protruded up from the floor. As always, Alex was unable to remember which was which. But even from a distance there was something menacing about the place. It was like looking into the open mouth of some giant, undersea monster. He could almost imagine the stalactites and stalagmites biting down, the whole thing swallowing him up.

But he had to go in. The cave wasn't very deep and apart from the rock formations it was empty, with a wide, sandy floor. He was thankful for that. Swimming too far into an underwater cave, at sunset, on his own, really would have been madness. He could see the back wall from the entrance – and there were the first of the metal rungs! They were dark red now and covered in green slime and coral, but they were clearly man-made, disappearing up the far wall and presumably continuing all the way to the top of the Devil's Chimney. There was no sign of Turner or Troy. Had the two agents decided to climb up after all? Should Alex try to climb after them?

Alex was about to swim forward when there was another movement just outside his field of vision. Whatever he had seen before had come back, swimming the other way. Puzzled, he looked up. And froze. He actually felt the air stop somewhere at the back of his throat. The last of the bubbles chased each other up to the surface. Alex just hung there, fighting for control. He wanted to scream. But underwater, it isn't possible to scream.

He was looking at a great white shark, at least three metres long, circling slowly above him. The sight was so unreal, so utterly shocking, that at first Alex quite literally didn't believe his eyes.

It had to be an illusion, some sort of trick. The very fact that it was so close to him seemed impossible. He stared at the white underbelly, the two sets of fins, the down-turned crescent mouth with its jagged, razor-sharp teeth. And there were the deadly, round eyes, as black and as evil as anything on the planet. Had they seen him yet?

Alex forced himself to breathe. His heart was pounding. Not just his heart – his whole body. He could hear his breath, as if amplified, in his head. His legs hung limp beneath him, refusing to move. He was terrified. That was the simple truth. He had never been so scared in his life.

What did he know about sharks? Was the great white going to attack him? What could he do? Desperately, Alex tried to draw on what little knowledge he had.

There were three hundred and fifty known species of shark but only very few of them were known to have attacked people. The great white – *carcharodon carcharias* – was definitely one of them. Not so good. But shark attacks were rare. Only about a hundred people were killed every year. More people died in car accidents. On the other hand, the waters around Cuba were notoriously dangerous. This was a single shark...

...still circling him, as if choosing its moment...

...and it might not have seen him. No. That wasn't possible. A shark's eyes are ten times more sensitive than a human being's. Even in pitch darkness it can see eight metres away. And anyway, it doesn't need eyes. It has receptors built into its snout which can detect even the tiniest electrical current. A beating heart, for example.

Alex tried to force himself to calm down. His own heart was generating minute amounts of electricity. His terror would guide the creature towards him. He had to relax!

What else? Don't splash. Don't make any sudden movements. Advice given to him by Ian Rider came echoing back across the years. A shark will be attracted to shiny metal objects, to brightly coloured clothes, and to fresh blood. Alex slowly turned his head. His oxygen cylinder had been painted black. His T-shirt was white. There was no blood. Was there?

He turned his hands over, examining himself. And then he saw it. Just above the wrist on his left arm. There was a small gash. He hadn't even noticed it, but now he remembered catching his wrist on the side of the boat as he fell backwards. A tiny amount of blood, brown rather than red, twisted upwards out of the wound.

Tiny, but enough. A shark can smell one drop of blood in twenty-five gallons of water. Who had taught him that? He had forgotten, but he knew it was true. The shark had smelled him...

...and was still smelling him, slowly closing in...

The circles were getting smaller. The shark's fins were down. Its back was arched. And it was moving in a strange, jerky pattern. The three textbook signs of an imminent attack. Alex knew that he had only seconds between life and death. Slowly, trying not to make any disturbance in the water, he reached down. The knife was still there, strapped to his leg, and he carefully unfastened it. The weapon would be tiny against the bulk of the great white and the blade would seem pathetic compared to those vicious teeth. But Alex felt better having it in his hand. It was something.

He looked around him. Apart from the cave itself, there was nowhere to hide – and the cave was useless. The mouth was too wide. If he went inside, the shark would simply follow him. And yet, if he made it to the ladder, he might be able to climb it. That would take him out of the water – up the Devil's Chimney and onto dry land. True, he would surface in the middle of the Casa de Oro.

But no matter how bad General Sarov might be, he couldn't be worse than the shark.

He had made his decision. Slowly, keeping the shark in his sight, he began to move towards the cave's entrance. For a moment he thought the shark had lost interest in him. It seemed to be swimming away. But then he saw that he had been tricked. The creature turned and, as if fired from a gun, rushed through the water, heading straight for him. Alex dived down, air exploding from his lungs. There was a boulder to one side of the cave and he tried to wedge himself into a corner, putting it between himself and his attacker. It worked. The shark curved away. At that moment, Alex lunged forward with the knife. He felt his arm shudder as the blade cut into the thick hide just under the two front fins. As the shark flickered past, he saw that it was leaving a trail of what looked like brown smoke. Blood. But he knew that he had barely wounded it. He had managed a pinprick, nothing more. And he had probably angered it, making it all the more determined.

Worse, he was bleeding more himself. In his attempt to get out of the way, he had backed into the coral, which had cut his arms and legs. Alex felt no pain. That would come later. But now he really had done it. He had advertised himself: dinner, fresh and bleeding. It was a miracle that the great white hadn't been joined by a dozen friends.

He had to get into the cave. The shark was some distance away, out to sea. The cave entrance was just a few metres away to his left. Two or three kicks and he would be in – then through the stalactites and stalagmites and onto the ladder. Could he do it in time?

Alex kicked with all his strength. At the same time he was thrashing with his hands and cursed noiselessly as he accidentally dropped the knife. Well, it would do him no good anyway. He kicked a second time. The entrance to the cave loomed up in front of him. He was in front of it now but not inside...

...And he was too late! The shark came hurtling towards him. The eyes seemed to have grown bigger. The mouth was stretched open in a snarl that contained all the hatred in the world. Its mouth was gaping, the dreadful teeth slicing through the water. Alex jerked back-wards, twisting his spine. The shark missed him by centimetres. He felt the surge of water push-ing him away. Now the shark was in the cave, but he wasn't. It was turning to attack again, and this time it wouldn't be confused by the rock wall and the boulders. This time Alex was right in its sights.

And then it happened. Alex heard a metallic buzz and, in front of his eyes, the stalagmites rose out of the floor and the stalactites dropped out of the ceiling, teeth that skewered the shark not once, but five or six times. Blood exploded into the water. Alex saw the dreadful eyes as its head whipped from side to side. He could almost imagine the creature howling in pain. It was completely trapped, as if in the jaws of a monster even more dreadful than itself. How had it happened? Alex hung in the water, shocked and uncomprehending. Slowly the blood cleared. And he understood.

Turner and Troy had been wrong a second time. Sarov had known about the Devil's Chimney and he had made sure that nobody could reach it by swimming through the cave. The stalagmites and stalactites were fake. They were made of metal, not stone, and were mounted on some sort of hydraulic spring. Swimming into the cave, the shark must have activated an infra-red beam which in turn had triggered the ambush. Even as he watched, the deadly spears retracted, sliding back into the floor and ceiling. There was a hum and the body of the shark was sucked into the cave, disappearing into a trap. So the place even had its own disposal system! Alex was beginning to understand the nature of the man who lived in the Casa de Oro. Whatever else he might be, Sarov left nothing to chance.

And now he knew what had happened to the two CIA agents. Alex felt sick. All he wanted to do was get away. Not just out of the water but out of the country. He wished he had never come.

There was still a lot of blood in the water. Alex swam quickly, afraid that it would attract more sharks. But he paced himself, carefully measuring his ascent towards the surface. If a diver rises too quickly, nitrogen gets trapped in the blood-stream causing the painful and potentially lethal sickness known as the bends. That was the last thing Alex needed right now. He spent five minutes at three metres' depth – a final safety stop – then came up for air. The whole world had changed while he had been underwater. The sun had rolled behind the horizon and the sky, the sea, the land, the very air itself had become suffused with the deepest crimson. He could see Garcia's boat, a dark shadow, about twenty metres away and swam over to it. Suddenly he was cold. His teeth were chattering – although they had probably been chattering from the moment he had seen the shark.

Alex reached the side of the boat. Garcia was still sitting on the deck with a cigarette between his lips but didn't offer to help him out.

"Thanks a bunch," Alex muttered.

He slipped off his BCD – the oxygen tank came with it – and heaved it onto the boat, then pulled himself out of the water. He winced. Out of the water, he could feel the wounds that the coral had inflicted on his limbs. But there was no time to do anything about that now. As soon as he was standing on the deck, he unhooked his weight belt and dumped it to one side along with his mask and snorkel. There was a towel in Turner's bag. He took it out and used it to rub himself dry. Then he went over to Garcia.

"We have to go," he said. "Turner and Troy are dead. The cave is a trap. Do you understand? You have to take me back to the hotel."

Garcia still said nothing. For the first time, Alex noticed something about the cigarette in the man's mouth. It wasn't actually lit. Suddenly uneasy, Alex reached out. Garcia fell forward. There was a knife sticking out of his back.

Alex felt something hard touch him between his shoulder blades and a voice, which seemed to have trouble with the words it was saying, whispered from somewhere behind him.

"A little late to be out swimming, I think. I advise you now to keep very still."

A speedboat which had been lurking in the shadows on the other side of the diving boat roared to life, lights blazing. Alex stood where he was. Two more men climbed onboard, both of them speaking in Spanish. He just had time to glimpse the dark, grinning face of one of Sarov's *macheteros* before a sack was thrown over his head. Something touched his arm and he felt a sting and knew that he had just been injected with a hypodermic syringe. Almost at once, the strength went out of his legs and he would have collapsed but for the invisible hands that held him up.

And then he was lifted up and carried away. Alex began to wonder if it would have made any difference if the shark had reached him after all. The men who were carrying him off the boat were treating him like someone who was already dead.

THE CRUSHER

Alex couldn't move.

He was lying on his back on a hard, sticky surface. When he tried to raise his shoulders, he felt
his T-shirt clinging to whatever it was underneath
him. It was as if he had been glued into place.
Whatever had been injected into him had removed
all power of movement from his arms and legs. The
bag still covered his head, keeping him in darkness. He knew that he had been loaded into the
speedboat and taken back to the coast. Some sort
of van had met him and brought him here. He had
heard footsteps and rough hands had grabbed
him, carrying him like a sack of vegetables. He
guessed that three or four men had been involved
in the journey, but they had barely spoken. Once
he had heard the same man who had spoken to

him on the boat. He had muttered a couple of words in Spanish. But his voice was so indistinct, the words so garbled, that Alex had found it hard to understand what he was saying.

Fingers brushed against the side of his neck and suddenly the bag was removed. Alex blinked. He was lying in a brightly lit warehouse or factory; the first thing he saw was the metal framework supporting the roof, with arc lamps hanging down. The walls were bare brick, white-washed, the floor lined with terracotta tiles. There was machinery on both sides of him. Most of it looked agricultural and a hundred years out of date. There were chains and buckets and a compli-cated pulley system that fed into a series of metal wheels that could have come out of a giant antique watch, and next to them, a pair of earthenware cauldrons. Alex twisted round and saw more caul-drons on the other side and, in the distance, some sort of filtration system with pipes leading every-where. He realized now that he was lying on a long conveyor belt. He tried once again to get up or even roll off, but his body wouldn't obey him.

A man stepped into his line of vision.

Alex looked up into a pair of eyes that weren't actually quite a pair. They weren't positioned correctly in the man's face and one of them was bloodshot. Alex wondered if it could even see. The man had been horribly injured at some time. He was bald on one side of his head, but not on the other. His mouth was slanting. His skin was dead. In a beauty contest, he wouldn't even come a close second to the great white shark.

There were a couple of dark, unsmiling workers standing behind him. They were shabbily dressed, with moustaches and bandanas. Neither of them spoke. They seemed keenly interested in what was about to happen.

"Your name?" The movements of the man's mouth didn't quite match what he was saying, so seeing him speak was a bit like watching a badly dubbed film.

"Alex Gardiner," Alex said.

"Your real name?"

"I just told you."

"You lied. Your real name is Alex Rider."

"Why ask if you think you know?"

The man nodded as if Alex had asked a fair question. "My name is Conrad," he said. "We have met before."

"Have we?" Alex tried to think. Then he remembered. The man he had seen limping down the boardwalk in Miami wearing sunglasses and a straw hat! It was the same man.

Conrad leaned forward. "Why are you here?" he asked.

"I'm on vacation with my mom and dad." Alex decided it was time to pretend he was just an ordinary fourteen year old. "Where are they?" he demanded. "Why have you brought me here? What happened to the man on the boat? I want to go home!"

"Where is your home?" Conrad asked.

"I live in LA. De Flores Street, west Hollywood."

"No." There was no doubt at all in Conrad's voice. "Your accent is very convincing, but you are not American. You are English. The people you came with were called Tom Turner and Belinda Troy. They were agents of the CIA. They are now dead."

"I don't know what you're talking about. You've got the wrong guy."

Conrad smiled. At least, one side of his mouth smiled. The other could only manage a slight twitch. "Lying to me is stupid and a waste of time. I have to know why you are here," he said. "It is an unusual experience to interrogate a child, but it is one I shall enjoy. You are the only one left. So tell me, Alex Rider, why did you come to Cayo Esqueleto? What were you planning to do?"

"I wasn't planning to do anything!" Despite everything, Alex thought it was worth one last try. He was still speaking with an American accent. "My dad's a film producer. He's got nothing to do with the CIA. Who are you? And why have you brought me here?"

"I am losing my patience!" Conrad took a break, as if the effort of talking was too much for him. "Tell me what I want to know."

"I'm on vacation!" Alex said. "I've already told you!"

"You have told me lies. Now you will tell me the truth."

Conrad leaned down and picked up a large metal box with two buttons – one red, one green – attached to a thick cable. He pressed the green button. At once, Alex felt a jolt underneath him. An alarm bell rang. Somewhere in the distance there was a loud whine as a machine started up. A few seconds later, the conveyor began to move.

Using all his strength, Alex fought against the drug that was in his system, forcing his head up so that he could look over his feet. What he saw sent a spasm of shock all the way through him. His head swam and he thought he was going to faint. The conveyor belt was carrying him towards two huge, spinning grindstones about seven metres away. They were so close to each other they were almost touching. There was one underneath and one on top. The belt stopped just at the point where they met. Alex was slumped helplessly on the belt. There was nothing he could do. He was moving towards the grindstones at a rate of about ten centimetres a second. It would take him a little over a minute to reach them. When he did finally get there, he would be crushed. That was the death that this man had arranged for him.

"Do you know how sugar was produced?" Conrad asked. "This place, where you are now, is a sugar mill. The machinery used to be steam-powered but now it is electric. The sugar cane was delivered here by the *colonos* – the farmers. It was shredded and then placed on a belt to be crushed. After that it was filtered. Water was allowed to evaporate. Then the remaining syrup was placed in cauldrons and heated so that it formed crystals." Conrad paused to draw breath. "You, Alex, are at the beginning of that process. You are about to be fed into the crusher. I ask you to imagine the pain that lies ahead of you. Your toes will enter first. Then you will be sucked in one centimetre at a time. After your toes, your feet. Your legs and your knees. How much of you will pass through before you are allowed the comfort of death? Think about it! Whatever else it is, I can promise you that it will not be sweet."

Conrad raised the box with the two buttons. "Tell me what I want to know and I will press the red button. It stops the machine."

"You're wrong!" Alex shouted. "You can't do this!"

"I am doing this. And I am never wrong. Please, do not waste any more time. You have so little of it left..."

Alex lifted his head up again. The grindstones were getting closer with every second that passed. He could feel their vibration, transmitted down the conveyor belt.

"How much did the agents know?" Conrad demanded. "Why were they here?"

Alex slumped back. The pounding of the two stones enveloped him. He looked past Conrad at the other two men. Would they let him do this? But their faces were impassive. "Please...!" he shouted. Then stopped himself. There was no mercy in this man. He had seen that at once. He gritted his teeth, biting back his fear. He wanted to cry. He could actually feel the tears in his eyes. This wasn't what he wanted. He had never asked to be a spy. Why should he be expected to die like one?

"You have perhaps fifty seconds more," Conrad said.

And that was when Alex made up his mind. There was no point in going silently to this bloody and unspeakable death. This wasn't a World War Two film with him as the hero. He was a schoolboy and everyone – Blunt, Mrs Jones, the CIA – had lied to him and played tricks on him to get him here. Anyway, Conrad already knew who he was. He had called him by his real name. Conrad knew that Troy and Turner had been American spies. There was only one piece of information he could add. The CIA were looking for a nuclear bomb. And why shouldn't he tell Conrad that? Maybe it would be enough to stop him using it.

"They were searching for a bomb!" he cried out. "A nuclear bomb. They know Sarov bought uranium from the Salesman. They came here with a Geiger counter. They were going to break into the villa and look for the bomb."

"How did they know?"

"I don't know..."

"Thirty seconds."

The rumbling and pounding was louder than ever. Alex looked up and saw the stones less than three metres away. Air was rushing between them and flowing over him. He could feel the breeze cold on his skin. The fact that he wasn't tied down, that his arms and legs were free, only made it all the worse. He couldn't move! The drug had turned him into a piece of living meat on its way to the mincer. Perspiration flowed down the side of his face then followed the line of his jaw and curved behind his neck.

"It was Turner!" Alex yelled. "He found out from the Salesman. He was working undercover. They found out that he'd sold you the uranium and they came here looking for the bomb."

"Did they know the purpose of the bomb?"

"No! I don't know. They didn't tell me. Now stop the machine and let me go."

Conrad considered for a moment. The box was still in his hand.

"No," he said. "I don't think so."

"What?" Alex screamed the single word. He could barely hear himself above the noise of the grindstones.

"You've been a bad boy," Conrad said. "And bad boys have to be punished."

"But you said—"

"I lied. Just like you. But of course I must kill you. You are of no further use..."

Alex went mad. He opened his mouth and screamed, trying to find the strength to separate himself from the conveyor belt. His brain knew what it wanted. His body refused to obey. It was useless. He jerked upwards. His feet were moving ever closer to the spinning stones. Conrad took a step back. He was going to watch as Alex was fed through the crusher. The two workers behind him would clear up when it was over.

"No!" Alex howled.

"Goodbye, Alex," Conrad said.

And then – another voice. In another language. One that Alex didn't understand.

Conrad said something. Alex could no longer hear. The man's lips moved but any sound was snatched away by the roar of the machine.

Alex's bare toes were being battered by the wind that was forced through the stones. They were five centimetres away from being crushed. Four centimetres, three centimetres, two centimetres...

There was a gunshot.

Sparks. The smell of smoke.

The grindstones were still spinning. But the conveyor belt had stopped. Alex's feet were jutting over the end of the belt. He could almost feel the spinning stone racing past his toes.

Then the voice came again, speaking now in English.

"My dear Alex. I'm so sorry. Are you all right?"

Alex tried to reply with the worst swear-word he knew. But it wouldn't come. He couldn't even breathe.

With a sense of gratitude, he passed out.

"You will have to forgive Conrad. He is an excellent assistant and useful in so many ways. But he can also be a little ... over-enthusiastic."

Alex had woken up in the most magnificent bedroom he had ever seen. He was lying on a four poster bed opposite a floor-to-ceiling mirror in an ornate gold frame. All the furniture in the room was antique and wouldn't have been out of place in a museum. There was a painted chest at the foot of the bed, a massive wardrobe with elaborately carved doors, a chandelier with five curving arms. The shutters on the windows had been folded back to reveal a wrought iron balustrade looking out over a courtyard.

The man, who had introduced himself as General Alexei Sarov, was sitting on a chair next to the mirror, dressed in a dark suit. His legs were crossed. His back was completely straight. Alex examined the face with its grey hair and intelligent blue eyes. He recognized his voice from the sugar mill and knew – without knowing why – that it was the general who had saved him.

It was dark outside. Alex guessed it must be after midnight. Someone had dressed him in a white nightshirt that came down to his knees. He wondered how long he had been asleep. And how long the Russian had been waiting for him to wake up.

"Do you want something to eat?" That had been his first question.

"No, thank you. I'm not hungry."

"A drink then?"

"Some water..."

"I have some here."

The water came in a silver jug, served in a gleaming crystal glass. General Sarov poured it himself, then handed it to Alex. Alex reached out, grateful that the drug Conrad had pumped into him had worn off while he was asleep and that he could move his arms again. He sipped. The water was ice-cold. That was when Sarov began his apology, speaking in faultless English.

"Conrad had no orders to eliminate you. On the contrary, when I found out who you were, I very much wanted to meet you."

Alex wondered about that, but decided to ignore it for the moment. "How did you find out who I was?" he asked. There seemed no point in denying it now.

"We have a very sophisticated security system both here and in Havana." The general seemed uninterested in explaining more. "I'm afraid you've had a terrible ordeal."

"The people I came here with had a worse one."

Again the general raised a hand, brushing aside the details. "Your friends are dead. Were they your friends, Alex?" A brief pause. "I was of course perfectly well aware of the Devil's Chimney when I first moved into the Casa de Oro. I had a simple defence mechanism constructed. Diving is prohibited on this side of the island so when the occasional diver is foolish enough to enter the cave, he is only paying the price of his curiosity. They tell me that a shark was killed there..."

"It was a great white."

"You saw it?"

Alex said nothing. Sarov raised his hands, resting his chin on the tip of his fingers.

"You are as remarkable as I was told," he continued. "I have read your file, Alex. You have no parents. You were raised by an uncle who was himself a spy. You were trained by the Special Air Service, the SAS, and sent on your first mission in the south of England. And then, just a few weeks later, to France... Some would say that you have had the luck of the devil, but I do not personally believe in the devil – or in God, for that matter. But I believe in you, Alex. You are quite unique."

Alex was getting tired of all this flattery. And he couldn't help but feel that there was something sinister in it. "Why am I here?" he asked.

"What do you want with me?"

"Why you are here should be self-evident," Sarov answered. "Conrad wanted to kill you. I prevented him. But I cannot allow you to return to the hotel or, indeed, to leave the island. You will have to consider yourself my prisoner, although if the Casa de Oro is a prison, I hope you will find it a comfortable one. As to what I want with you..." Sarov smiled to himself, his eyes suddenly distant. "It is late," he announced suddenly. "We can talk about that tomorrow."

He stood up.

"Is it true that you have a nuclear bomb?" Alex asked.

"Yes."

Part of the puzzle fell into place. "You bought uranium from the Salesman. But then you ordered Conrad to kill him! You blew up his boat!"

"That is correct."

So Alex had been right all along. He had seen Conrad in Miami. Conrad had put some sort of explosive device on the *Mayfair Lady* – and it was that, not the fire, that had caused the destruction and loss of life. Turner and Troy had accused him unfairly.

"The nuclear bomb..." Alex said. "What are you going to do with it?"

"Are you afraid?"

"I want to know."

The general considered. "I will tell you only this for now," he said. "I do not imagine that you know a great deal about my country, Alex. The Union of Soviet Socialist Republics as it was once called. The USSR. Russia, as it is today. I do not suppose these things are taught to you in your Western schools."

"I know that communism is finished, if that's what you mean," Alex said. "And it's a bit late for a history lesson."

"My country was once a world power," Sarov continued, ignoring him. "It was one of the most powerful nations on the earth. Who put the first man into space? We did! Who made the greatest advances in science and technology? Who was feared by the rest of the world?" He paused. "You are right. Yes. Communism has been driven out. And what do you see in its place?" A flicker of anger appeared on his face – there only for a second and then it was gone. "Russia has become second-rate. There is no law and order. The prisons are empty and criminals control the streets. Millions of Russians are addicted to drugs. Millions more have AIDS. Women and children find work as prostitutes. And all this so that the people can eat McDonald's and buy Levi jeans and talk on their mobile telephones in Red Square!"

General Sarov walked over to the door.

"You ask me what I am going to do," he said. "I am going to turn back the page and undo the damage of the last thirty years. I am going to give my country back its pride and its position on the world stage. I am not an evil man, Alex. Whatever your superiors may have told you, my only wish is to stop the disease and to make the world a better place. I hope you can believe that. It matters very much to me that you should come to see things my way."

"You have a nuclear bomb," Alex said, speaking slowly. "I don't understand. How is that going to help you achieve what you want?"

"That will be revealed to you … in time. Let us have breakfast together at nine o'clock. Then I will show you around the estate."

General Sarov nodded and left the room.

Alex waited a minute before slipping out of bed. He looked out into the courtyard, then went and tried the door. He wasn't surprised by what he found. Sarov had described the Casa de Oro as a prison and he was right. There was no way Alex could climb down into the courtyard. And the bedroom door was locked.

THE HOUSE OF SLAVES

A knock at the door woke Alex just after eight o'clock the next morning. As he sat up in bed, a woman dressed in black with a white apron came in, carrying a case which he recognized as his own. Sarov must have sent someone to the Hotel Valencia to collect it. Alex waited until the woman had gone, then got quickly out of bed and opened it. All his clothes were there. So were the Michael Owen figurine and the bubblegum that Smithers had given him. Only the mobile phone had gone. Clearly, Sarov didn't want him to phone home.

After what Sarov had said the night before, he decided to leave his Levi's in the case. Instead he chose a pair of baggy shorts, a plain T-shirt and the Reefer sandals he'd last used when he was surfing in Cornwall. He got dressed and went over to the window. The courtyard he had seen the night before was now bathed in sunlight. It was rectangular in shape, surrounded by a marble walkway and a series of arched colonnades. Two servants were sweeping the fine sand which covered the ground. Two more were watering the plants. He looked up and saw the watch tower that he had noticed from the boat. There was still a guard in place, his machine-gun clearly visible.

At ten to nine, the door opened again. This time it was Conrad who came in, wearing a black shirt buttoned to the neck, black trousers and sandals that revealed four toes on one foot, only three on the other.

"*Desayuno!*" Alex recognized the Spanish word for breakfast. Conrad had spat the single word out as if it offended him to say it. He was clearly unhappy to see Alex again – but then of course, he'd had other plans.

"Good morning, Conrad!" Alex forced a smile to his face. After what had happened the night before, he was determined to show that the man didn't scare him. He pointed. "You seem to have forgotten some of your toes."

He walked over to the door. As he passed through into the corridor, Conrad was suddenly close to him. "It isn't over yet," he whispered. "The general may change his mind."

Alex continued forward. He found himself in a wide corridor above a second courtyard. He looked down at a stone fountain surrounded by white pillars. He could smell perfume in the air. The sound of water rippled through the house. Conrad pointed and Alex took a staircase down and into a room where breakfast had already been served.

General Sarov was sitting at a huge polished table, eating a plate of fruit. He was wearing a tracksuit. He smiled as Alex came in, and gestured towards an empty seat. There were a dozen to choose from.

"Good morning, Alex. You will have to forgive my clothes. I always run before breakfast. Three times around the plantation. A distance of twenty-four miles. I'll change later. Did you sleep well?"

"Yes, thank you."

"Help yourself, please, to breakfast. There is fruit and cereal. Fresh bread. Eggs. Personally, I eat my eggs raw. This is a habit I have followed throughout my life. To cook food is to remove half its goodness. Up in smoke!" He raised a hand in the air. "Man is the only creature on the planet that needs to have his meat and vegetables burned or broiled before he can consume them. However, if you wish, I can have some eggs prepared the way you like."

"No thanks, General. I'll stick with the fruit and cereal."

Sarov noticed Conrad standing at the door. "I don't need you now, thank you, Conrad. We'll meet again at midday."

Conrad's one good eye narrowed. He nodded and left the room.

"I'm afraid Conrad doesn't like you," Sarov said.

"That's all right. I'm not crazy about Conrad." Alex glanced at the door. "What exactly is the matter with him?" he asked. "He doesn't look well."

"By any rights, he should be dead. He was involved in an explosion with a bomb which he happened to be carrying at the time. Conrad is something of a scientific miracle. There are more than thirty metal pins in his body. He has a metal plate in his skull. There are metal wires in his jaw and in most of his major joints."

"He must set off a lot of alarms in airports," Alex muttered.

"I would advise you not to make fun of him,

Alex. He still very much hopes to kill you." Sarov touched his lips with a napkin. "I won't allow it to happen, but while we are discussing such unpleasant matters, perhaps I should lay down some house rules, so to speak. I have removed the mobile telephone which I found in your case and I should tell you that all the phones in the house require a code before they can be used. You are to make no contact with the outside world."

"My people may worry about me," Alex said.

"From what I know of Mr Blunt and his colleagues in London, that is unlikely. But it's unimportant. By the time they begin to ask questions, it will be too late."

Too late? Why? Alex realized he was still completely in the dark.

"The Casa de Oro is fenced all around. The fence is electrified. There is only one entrance and it is well guarded. Do not attempt to escape, Alex. If you do, you may be shot and that is not at all what I have planned. After today, I'm afraid I will be moving you to new quarters. As you may well be aware, I have important guests arriving and it would be better for you to 'have your own space' as I believe you say. You are still welcome to use the house, the pool, the grounds. But I would ask you to remain invisible. My guests speak very little English so there is no point approaching them. If you cause me any embarrassment, I will have you whipped."

General Sarov reached forward and pronged a slice of pineapple.

"But that's enough of this unpleasantness," he said. "We have the whole morning together. Do you ride?"

Alex hesitated. He didn't like horse-riding. "I have ridden," he said.

"Excellent."

Alex helped himself to some melon. "I asked you last night what you wanted with me," he said. "You still haven't given me a reply."

"All in good time, Alex. All in good time."

After breakfast, they walked out into the open air. Now Alex understood how the house had got its name. It was made of some sort of pale yellow brick that, with the sun beating down, really did look gold. Although the house was only two storeys high, it was spread over a vast area, with wide stone steps leading down to a formal garden. Blunt had described it as a palace, but it was more elegant than majestic with slender doors and windows, more archways and finely carved balustrades. Looking at the house, it was as if nothing had changed since the early nineteenth century when it had been built. But there were also armed guards on patrol. There were alarm bells and a series of spotlights mounted on metal brackets. Ugly reminders of the modern age.

They continued over to a stable block where a man was waiting with two magnificent horses; a white stallion for Sarov, a smaller grey for Alex. Riding was the one sport that Alex had never enjoyed. The last time he had got onto a horse it had almost killed him, and it was with reluctance that he took hold of the reins and swung himself into the saddle. Out of the corner of his eye he saw Sarov do the same and knew at once that the Russian was an expert, in total control of his steed.

They rode out together, Alex trying to keep his balance and not look too out of control. Fortunately, his horse seemed to know where they were going.

"This was a sugar farm once," Sarov explained, repeating what Troy had already told him. "Slaves worked here. There were almost a million slaves in Cuba and Cayo Esqueleto." He pointed at the tower. "That was the watch tower. They would ring a bell there at half past four in the morning for the slaves to start work. They were brought here from West Africa. They worked here. And they died here."

They passed close to a low, rectangular building some way from the main house. Alex noticed that the single door and all the windows were barred.

"That is the *barracón*," Sarov said. "The house of slaves. Two hundred of them slept in there, penned in like animals. If we have time, I will show you the punishment block. We still have the original stocks. Can you imagine, Alex, being fastened by your ankles for weeks, or even months at a time? Unable to move. Starving and thirsty..."

"I don't want to imagine it," Alex said.

"Of course not. The Western world prefers to forget the crimes that made it rich."

Alex was relieved when they broke into a canter. At least it meant there was no further need to talk. They followed a dirt track that brought them to the edge of the sea. Looking down, Alex could see where Garcia's boat had been moored the day before. It reminded him of the true nature of the man he was with. Sarov was being friendly. He evidently enjoyed having Alex as his guest. But he was a killer. And a killer with a nuclear bomb.

They came to the end of the track and continued more slowly now, with the sea on their right.

The Casa de Oro had disappeared behind them.

"I wish to tell you something about myself," Sarov said suddenly. "In fact, I will tell you more than I have ever told anyone else."

He rode on for a few moments in silence.

"I was born in 1940," he began. "This was during the Second World War, the year before the Germans attacked my country. Perhaps that is why I have always been a patriot, why I have always thought my country should come first. I have spent much of my life serving it. In the army, fighting for what I believe in. I still believe I am serving it now."

He reined in his horse and turned to Alex, who had stopped beside him.

"I got married when I was thirty. A year later, my wife gave me something I had always wanted. A son. His name was Vladimir and from the moment he drew his first breath he was the best thing in my life. He grew into a handsome boy, and let me tell you, no father could have been prouder than I was of him. He did well at school, top in almost every class. He was a first-class athlete. I think he could one day have competed at Olympic level. But that was not to be..."

Alex already knew the end of this story. He remembered what Blunt had told him.

"I believed it was right for Vladimir to serve his country, just as I had," Sarov went on. "I wanted him to join the army. His mother disagreed. Unfortunately, that disagreement ended our marriage."

"You asked her to leave?"

"No. I didn't ask her to leave. I ordered her to. She departed from my house and I never saw her again. And Vladimir did join the army. This was in 1988 when he was sixteen years old. He was flown to Afghanistan where we were fighting a hard, difficult war. He had been there for just three weeks when he was sent to reconnoitre a village as part of a patrol. A sniper shot him and he died."

Sarov's voice cracked briefly and he stopped. But a moment later he continued in a careful, measured tone.

"The war ended a year later. Our government, weak and cowardly, had lost the spirit to fight. We withdrew. The whole thing had been for nothing. And this is what you must understand. This is the truth. There is nothing more terrible in this world than for a father to lose his son." He took a breath. "I believed I had lost Vladimir for ever. Until I met you."

"Me?" Alex was almost too startled to speak.

"You are just two years younger than Vladimir was when he died. But you have so much in common with him, Alex – even though you were brought up on the other side of the world! There is, first, a very slight resemblance. But it is not just your physical appearance. You too are serving your country. Fourteen years old and a spy! How rare it is to find any young person who is prepared to fight for his beliefs!"

"Well, I wouldn't go that far," Alex muttered.

"You have courage. That business at the sugar factory and in the cave would prove it even if your track record didn't speak volumes more. You speak many languages and one day, soon, you could learn Russian. You ride, you dive, you fight, and you aren't scared. I have never met a boy like you. Except one. You are like my Vladimir, Alex, and that is what I hope you will become."

"What are you getting at?" Alex asked. They still weren't moving and he was beginning to feel the heat of the sun. The horse was sweating and attracting flies. The sea was a long way beneath them and none of its breeze was reaching them.

"Isn't it obvious? I've read your file. You have grown up on your own. You had an uncle but you didn't even know what he was until he died. You have no parents. I have no son. We are both alone."

"We're a world apart, General."

"We don't need to be. I am planning something

that will change the world for ever. When I am finished, the world will be a better, stronger, healthier place. You came here to prevent that happening. But when you understand what I'm doing, you will see that we do not need to be enemies. On the contrary! I want to adopt you!"

Alex stared. He didn't know what to say.

"You will be my son, Alex, and you will continue where Vladimir left off. I will be a father to you and we will share the new world I create. Don't speak now! Just consider. If I really believed you were my enemy, I would have allowed Conrad to kill you. But the moment I found out who you were, I knew that you couldn't be. We even have the same name, you and I. Alexei and Alex. I will adopt you, Alex. I will become the father you have lost."

"And what if I say no?"

"You will not say no!" Violence had slid into his eyes like smoke behind glass. His face was twisted as if in pain. Sarov took a deep breath and suddenly he was calm. "When you know the plan, you will join me."

"Then why don't you tell me the plan? Tell me what you're going to do!"

"Not yet, Alex. You're not ready yet. But you will be. And it will all happen very soon."

General Alexei Sarov pulled on his reins. The horse spun round and he galloped off, leaving the sea behind. Alex shook his head in wonderment. Then he kicked at the flanks of his own horse and followed.

That evening, Alex ate on his own. Sarov had excused himself, saying he had work to do. Alex didn't have much appetite. Conrad stood in the room watching his every mouthful and although he didn't speak, anger and hostility radiated out of him. The moment Alex finished, Conrad signalled, a single hand pointing to the door.

He followed Conrad out of the main house, down the steps and into the slave quarters, the *barracón* that Sarov had shown him earlier. It seemed that this was to be his new accommodation. The inside of the building was divided into a series of cells with bare brick walls and thick doors, each with a square grille in the centre. But at least it had been modernized. There was electricity, fresh water and – mercifully in the heat of the night – air-conditioning. Alex knew he was a lot luckier than the hundreds of lost souls who had once been confined there.

There was a basin and a toilet hidden behind a screen in his cell. Alex's case had been carried over and placed on a bed which had a metal frame and a thin mattress but which was still comfortable enough. Sarov had also provided him with books to read. Alex glanced at the covers. They were English translations of Russian classics; Tolstoy and Dostoevsky. He guessed they must have been Vladimir's favourite authors.

Conrad closed and locked the door.

"Goodnight, Conrad," Alex called out. "I'll call you if I need anything."

He just managed to glimpse a bloodshot eye peering through the grille and knew that he had scored a point. Then Conrad was gone.

Alex lay on the bed for some time, thinking about what Sarov had said. Adoption! It was almost too much for him to take in. Only a week ago he had wondered what it would be like to have a father, and now two of them had turned up at once – first Tom Turner and now Sarov! Things were definitely going from bad to worse.

There was a burst of light outside the window. Night had been replaced by a hard, electric daylight. Alex rolled off the bed and went over to the barred window. It looked out onto the main square at the front of the house. The electric lights he had noticed earlier had all come on and the square was full of people. The guards – a dozen of them – had formed a line, machine-guns resting against their chests. Servants and plantation workers had gathered around the door. Sarov himself was there, in a dark green uniform, several medals pinned to his chest. Conrad was behind him.

As Alex watched, four black limousines appeared, driving slowly along the lane that led up from the gatehouse. They were escorted by two motorcycles, the riders, like Sarov, in military dress. Dust spiralled behind the convoy, twisting up into the electric light.

They stopped. The car doors opened and about fifteen men got out. Alex could barely make out their faces against the blinding light. They were little more than silhouettes. But he saw one man – small, thin and bald, dressed in a suit. Sarov moved forward to meet him. The two men shook hands, then embraced. It was a signal for everyone to relax. Sarov gestured and the whole group began to move towards the house, leaving the motorcyclists behind.

Alex was certain he had seen the bald man before, in the newspapers. He knew now why he had been locked up in the slaves' quarters, out of harm's way. Whatever Sarov's plan was, the next phase had just begun.

The Russian president had arrived.

HEARTBEAT

Alex was let out of the slave house the following morning. It seemed he was going to be allowed to spend the day at liberty in the Casa de Oro ... although not on his own. An armed guard had been assigned to watch over him. The guard was in his twenties, roughly shaven. He spoke no English.

He led Alex first to breakfast, which he had on his own in the kitchen, not in the dining room where he had eaten with Sarov. While Alex ate, he stood at the door, watching him nervously, as if he was a firework that had just failed to go off.

"*Como se llama usted?*" Alex asked. *What's your name?*

"Juan..." The guard was reluctant to part with even that piece of information and answered the rest of Alex's questions with monosyllables or silence.

It was another blazing hot day. The island seemed to be caught in the grip of an endless summer. Alex finished his breakfast and went out into the main hall, where a few of the servants were, as ever, sweeping the floor or carrying supplies into the kitchen. The guards were still in place, up in the tower and around the perimeter. Alex made his way to the stables. He wondered if he would be allowed to go riding again and was pleasantly surprised when the guard brought out his grey for him, already saddled and prepared.

He set off a second time, with Juan just a few paces behind him on a chestnut mare. Alex didn't particularly want to go riding. His thighs and backside were still sore from the day before. But he was interested in the perimeter fence that Sarov had mentioned. He had said that it was electrified. But even electric fences sometimes pass trees that can be climbed. And Alex had already decided that he had to find a way out.

He still had no idea what Sarov was planning. He had talked of changing the world. Making it better, stronger, healthier. He obviously thought of himself as some sort of hero – but he was a hero armed with a nuclear bomb. As he rode across the long grass, Alex wondered what Sarov intended to do. His first thought was that the Russian was going to blow up an American city. Hadn't America once been Russia's greatest enemy? But that made no sense. Millions of people would die but it wouldn't change the world. Certainly not for the better. Could his target be somewhere in Europe? Or was he perhaps going to use the bomb to blackmail world governments into giving him what he wanted? That seemed more likely. But at the same time, Alex doubted it. Whatever he was planning in some way involved the Russian president.

I am going to turn back the page and undo the damage of the last thirty years.

Suddenly Alex knew that despite their childhood friendship, Sarov hated the Russian president and wanted to take his place. That was what this was all about. A new Russia that would once again be a world power. With Sarov at its head.

And he was going to achieve it with a single nuclear blast.

Alex had to escape. He had to tell the CIA that Turner and Troy had been killed and that Sarov did have a bomb. Once they knew that, they would take over. And he wanted to put as many kilometres between himself and the Casa de Oro as he could. Sarov's feelings for him, his desire to adopt him, bothered him as much as anything else. The old man was slightly mad. True, Sarov had saved his life. But it was Sarov who had put his life in danger in the first place. Despite the heat of the morning, Alex shivered. This whole adventure had turned into something that was rapidly spinning out of control.

They had reached the edge of the plantation, this time on the side away from the sea. And there, sure enough, was the fence – about five metres high, solid steel, with a smaller fence coming up to chest level on either side. There were large red signs with the single word PELIGRO printed in white letters. Even without the warning, the fence reeked of danger. There was a low humming that seemed to be coming from the ground. Alex noticed the charred and broken skeleton of a bird hanging on the wire. It must have flown into the fence and been killed instantly. Well, one thing was certain. He wasn't going to climb over. The fence stretched through grassland with barely a single tree in sight.

Alex turned his horse towards the bottom end of the plantation and the entrance gate. Maybe he would be able to find a way through there. It took them about half an hour to reach it, riding at walking pace. The fence continued all the way. The entrance was marked by a crumbling stone guardhouse with no glass in the windows and a

237

door hanging half off its hinges. There were two men inside and a third with a machine-gun standing beside a barrier. As Alex reached them, a car passed through. One of the limousines that he had seen the night before was leaving the compound. That gave him an idea. There was only one way out of here and that was in a car. Presumably the president's men would be making several journeys. That might give him a chance...

They rode back to the stables and dismounted. With Juan a few steps behind him, Alex walked back into the house. Almost at once he heard voices coming from the other side, and the splash of water. He crossed the inner courtyard past the fountain and went through an archway. There was a swimming pool on the other side, long and rect-angular, with palm trees growing on both sides, casting natural shadows over the tables and sun-loungers. In the distance he saw a newly con-structed tennis court. There were changing rooms, a sauna, an outside bar. From the back, the Casa de Oro looked like the playpen of a multi-millionaire.

Sarov was sitting at a table with the president, both of them holding drinks; water for Sarov, a cocktail for his guest. The president had changed into red shorts and a flowery short-sleeved shirt that hung loosely off his slight frame. There were four men standing close to him. It was obvious that they were the presidential bodyguard. The men were huge, dressed in black, with uniform sunglasses and a coil of wire disappearing into their ears. There was something almost ludicrous about the scene. The little man in his holiday clothes. The giant bodyguards. Alex looked at the pool. There were three strikingly attractive women sitting on the side, their feet dangling in the water. They were all in their twenties, wearing bikinis. They looked local. Alex was surprised to see them. He had thought Sarov too cold-blooded to enjoy such company. Or had they been invited here for the president?

Alex wondered if he was meant to be in this part of the grounds and was about to leave when Sarov saw him and waved a hand, calling him over. With a sense of growing curiosity, Alex walked over. Sarov spoke quickly to the president, who nodded and smiled.

"Good morning, Alex!" Sarov seemed unusually cheerful. "I understand you went out riding again. Please let me introduce you to my old friend, Boris Kiriyenko, the president of Russia. Boris, this is the boy I was telling you about."

The Russian president reached out and took Alex's hand. Alex could smell the alcohol on his breath. Whatever he was drinking in the cocktail, he'd had too much of it. "It is a pleasure," he said, in heavily accented English. He pointed a finger at Alex's face and broke into Russian. Alex heard the name Vladimir mentioned twice.

Sarov answered briefly, then translated for Alex. "He says that you remind him of my son." He smiled. "Would you like to swim, Alex? You look as if you need it."

Alex glanced at the three girls. "Unusual life-guards," he said.

Sarov laughed. "Some company for the president. He is, after all, on holiday, although unfortunately we do have a little work to do. Our local television station is naturally interested that we have such a distinguished visitor and Boris has agreed to give a brief interview. The crew will be here any minute now."

The president nodded but Alex wasn't sure if he'd understood.

"You can have the pool to yourself. We're going into Santiago after lunch, but I hope you'll join us for dinner, Alex. The chef has planned a special surprise for the main course."

There was a movement at the archway leading into the house. Conrad had appeared and with him was a short, serious-looking woman in a drab olive-green dress. There were two men behind her with cameras and lighting equipment.

"Ah! Here they are!" Sarov turned back to the president and suddenly Alex was forgotten.

He stripped to his swimming shorts and dived into the pool. After the long horse ride the water was cool and refreshing. He noticed the three girls watching him as he swam past. One of them winked at him and another giggled. Meanwhile, the camera crew was setting up its equipment in the shade of the palm trees. The Russian president waved a hand and one of his bodyguards brought over another cocktail. Alex was surprised that such an insignificant-looking man could be the head of a huge country. But then, he thought, most politicians are small and shabby, the sort of people who have been bullied at school. That's why they become politicians.

Alex put him out of his thoughts and concentrated on his swimming. In his mind he went over what Sarov had just said. They were driving into the city after lunch. That meant the cars would be leaving the compound. It was his only chance. Alex knew that there was no way off the island. The moment he was found missing, the alarm would be raised. Every guard at the airport would be on the lookout for him and he doubted he would be able to get on a boat. But if he could at least find a telephone that worked without an access code, he would be able to get in touch with the American mainland and they would send someone to pull him out.

He finished his eighth length and twisted round for a ninth. The Russian president was sitting in a chair, being wired for sound. Juan, Alex's personal guard, was waiting for him at the other end of the pool. Alex sighed. He was going to have to do something about Juan.

The television interview began. Sarov was watching carefully and, again, Alex got the impression that there was more to all this than met the eye.

He pulled himself out of the pool and went back to his quarters to get changed.

Alex wore another pair of shorts and an aertex shirt, both of them chosen because they were neutral colours, allowing him to blend in with the background. In his pocket he had a stick of the bubblegum that Smithers had given him. If everything went according to plan, he was going to need it.

Juan was standing outside the room. Alex was suddenly nervous about what he was going to do. After all, Sarov had already warned him what would happen if he tried to escape. He would be shot – or at the very least, whipped. But then he thought of the nuclear bomb. Sarov had to be stopped. His mind was made up.

He stopped suddenly and groaned. His whole face contorted with pain and he staggered to one side, putting out a hand to stop himself falling. Juan started forward, entering the room with a look of concern. At that moment, Alex straightened up. His foot shot out in a perfectly timed roundhouse kick that slammed into the soft flesh of the man's stomach. Juan didn't even cry out. With all the breath knocked out of him, he crumpled to the ground and lay still. Not for the first time, Alex thanked the five years' training that had given him a black belt – first grade *Dan* – in karate. Now he moved fast. He took the sheet off the bed and tore it into strips. He tied the man's hands and feet, then gagged him. Finally, he slipped out of the room, locking it behind him. It would be hours before the guard was found. By that time he would be away.

He came out of the *barracón*. The black limousines were still parked in front of the villa, waiting for the president and his men to leave. There was nobody in sight. Alex sprinted forward. Sarov had allowed him to wander around the

243

grounds of the plantation, but only if he was accompanied. If anyone saw him without his guard, they might guess what had happened. He reached the edge of the house and stopped, breathless, his back against the wall. Even the short run had made him sweat in the intense heat of the afternoon. He examined the cars. There were three of them. The one that had left earlier that morning still hadn't come back. The question was, when the president went into Santiago, which one would he take? Or would all three accompany him?

Alex was about to dart forward when he heard footsteps approaching round the side of the house. It was either guards or workers – the moment they turned the corner, they would see him. There was a narrow door to one side. He hadn't noticed it before. He fumbled for the handle. Fortunately, it wasn't locked. Just as two men in military dress appeared a few metres away, both armed, he slipped inside, closing the door behind him.

The chill of an air-conditioning system brushed over him. He looked around. He was in a part of the house that looked completely different to the rest. Here, the wooden floors and antique furniture had given way to a hi-tech, modern look. Halogen lighting led the way down a short corridor with glass doors on either side. Intrigued, Alex crept forward. He came to the first door and looked inside.

There were two technicians sitting gazing at a bank of TV screens. The room wasn't large and looked like an editing suite in a television studio. Alex eased the door open. There was no chance that the technicians would hear him. They were both wearing headphones, plugged into the machinery in front of them. Alex looked at the screens.

Every room in the main house was under observation. He recognized at once the room in which he had woken up. There was the kitchen, the dining room, the main courtyard with two of the president's men strolling across. He turned to another screen and stared. He was watching himself swimming lengths in the pool. That had been recorded too. And there was Sarov, sitting with his glass of water while, on the screen next to him, the president gave his interview to the crew that Alex had seen arrive.

It took Alex a moment to work out exactly what he was seeing. Everything was being recorded and edited. That was what the two technicians were doing now. The arrival of Boris Kiriyenko was playing on one screen. Next to it, the president emptied a glass of brandy, presumably the night before. On a third screen, the girls that Alex had seen at the swimming pool were introduced to him. They were simpering and smiling in low-cut dresses that left little to the imagination. Had he taken them to his room? If so, that would doubtless have been recorded too.

An image flickered. And there was the president giving his interview. One of the technicians must have been given the footage taken by the woman in the drab green dress. Kiriyenko was talking directly to the camera in the manner of a thousand politicians on *Newsnight* or *Panorama*. Totally serious – although he looked a little foolish in his flowery shirt. On the screen next to this one, the same Kiriyenko swam in the pool with one of the girls.

What did it all mean? Why did Sarov want this? Was the Casa de Oro nothing more than an elaborate, honeyed trap into which the president of Russia had unwittingly strayed?

Alex couldn't stay there any longer. Everything he saw made it more urgent for him to get out and warn the Americans. He was afraid he was going to miss the departure of the cars – and there wouldn't be a second chance.

He opened the door again and looked outside. The cars were still there but the guards had gone. He looked at his watch. It was two o'clock. If lunch hadn't finished already, it would do so shortly.

It had to be now! He ran forward to the nearest car and felt for the boot release. Was it going to be locked? His thumb found the silver button and pressed and, to his relief, the boot opened. It was a big car with plenty of room. He threw himself inside, then reached up and pulled the lid back down, locking it. At once he was trapped in pitch darkness and he had to force himself not to panic. It was like being buried alive. He tried to relax. This was going to work. Provided nobody opened the boot to put luggage in, he wouldn't be seen. The limousine would drive him out of the plantation and when they were parked in Santiago, he would make his escape.

Of course, the most difficult part was still to come. Alex couldn't see out of the car. He couldn't even see his own hand in front of his face. He was totally blind. He would simply have to guess when the driver and his passengers had gone and hope for the best. It was also impossible to open the boot from the inside. It was for this reason that Alex had brought along the gum. He would choose the moment and use the gum to blow his way out. With a bit of luck, he would slip away into the crowd before anyone realized what had happened.

But already he was wondering if this had been a good idea. It was hot inside the boot. He could imagine the sun beating down on the car, and realized that he had locked himself into an oven. Sweat was oozing out of every pore. His clothes were already sodden and he could hear it dripping onto the metal surface beneath him. How much air was there in the trunk? If Sarov didn't make a move soon, he'd have to blow the car open while it was still in the compound and face the consequences.

He fought down the panic and tried to breathe as shallowly as he could. His heart was thudding in his ears. He could feel the muscle hard at work in his chest as it pumped blood around his body. The veins in his neck and pulses were beating in rhythm. He wanted to stretch his legs but he didn't dare move in case he rocked the car. The minutes ticked by – and then he heard voices. There was the echoing clunk of a car door opening and the whole vehicle shifted from side to side as its passengers got in. Curled up in a foetal position, Alex waited for the boot to be thrown open, but it seemed that the president, or whoever was in the limousine, had decided not to bring any baggage. The car engine started up. Alex felt the vibrations and then, suddenly, they were moving, with Alex being jolted up and down as they started over the makeshift road.

After only about a minute they began to slow

down again and Alex knew that they must be approaching the gate and checkpoint. That was another worry. Would the guards search the car? But he had already seen one limousine leave the villa that morning, and although the guards had been there he hadn't seen anyone open the boot. The car had stopped. Alex didn't move. Everything was black. He heard voices as if in the far distance. Somebody shouted something but he couldn't make out a word they said. The car seemed to have been there for ever. Why was it taking so long? Get on with it! Alex was finding it harder and harder to breathe. It felt as if the air was already running out.

And then the car started forward and he let out a sigh of relief. He could imagine the barrier rising to let them through. The Casa de Oro would be behind them now. How far was it to Santiago? How would he know for sure when they were there?

The car stopped again.

The boot opened.

Cruel sunlight came rushing in. Alex blinked, putting a hand up to protect himself.

"Get out!" a voice said, in English.

Alex climbed out, soaking wet with his own perspiration. Sarov was standing in front of him. Conrad was next to him, holding an automatic pistol, not even trying to hide the pleasure in his eyes. Alex looked around. The car hadn't even left the compound. It had simply rolled forward and turned round. That had been the movement he had felt. There were two guards watching him, their faces blank. One of them was holding a device that looked a little like a megaphone, the sort teachers used at sports days. It was connected by a long wire to a box just inside the building.

"If you had wanted to visit Santiago, you had only to ask," Sarov said. "But I don't think you wanted to visit the city. I think you were running away."

Alex said nothing.

"Where is Juan?" Sarov asked.

Alex still didn't speak.

Sarov gazed at the boy. He seemed pained, as if he didn't understand why Alex had disobeyed him and didn't know quite what to do. "You disappoint me, Alex," he said, at length. "You were down at the cave. You saw the extent of my security arrangements there. Did you really think for a single minute that I would allow a car to drive in or out of this compound without knowing exactly who or what was inside?"

He suddenly reached out and took the megaphone device from the guard. He pointed it at

Alex's chest and pressed a button. At once, Alex heard a thumping sound that echoed through the air. It took him a second or two to realize that it was his own heart, amplified and transmitted out of speaker system hidden somewhere inside the guard house.

"The car was scanned at the barrier," Sarov explained. "Every car is scanned at the barrier, using the machine I am holding now. A sophisticated sensor. This is what the guard heard. You can hear it now."

Thud ... thud ... thud...

Alex listened to his own heart.

Sarov was suddenly angry. Nothing in his face had changed, but his pale blue eyes had turned to ice and there was a dreadful deadness about him, as if his own life had suddenly been drained away. "Do you not remember what I told you?" he whispered. "If you tried to escape, you would be shot. Conrad very much wishes to shoot you. He believes I am a fool to have you here as my guest. He is right."

Conrad stepped forward, the gun raised.

Thud ... thud ... thud ... thud...

Alex's heart was the animal inside him, beyond his control, responding to the fear he felt. There was nothing he could do to hide it. The heart was beating louder and faster, echoing out of the speakers.

"I don't understand you, Alex. Have you no idea what I'm offering you? Did you not hear a word that I said? I offer you my protection and you make an enemy of me! I want you to be my son, but you force me to destroy you instead."

Conrad touched the gun against Alex's heart.

Thudthudthudthudthudthudthud...

"Listen to the sound of your own terror. Do you hear it? And when you hear silence – it could be just a few seconds from now – that is when you will know you have died."

Conrad's finger tightened on the trigger.

Then Sarov turned off the sensor.

The heartbeat stopped.

Alex felt as if he had been shot. The sudden silence hit him like a hammer blow. Like a bullet from a gun. He fell to his knees, hollowed out, barely able to breathe. He knelt there in the dust, his hands at his sides. He no longer had the strength to stand up. Sarov looked at him and now there was only sadness in his face.

"He has learned his lesson," he said. "Take him back to his room."

He put down the sensor and, turning his back on the still kneeling boy, slowly climbed back into the car.

THE NUCLEAR DUSTBIN

At seven o'clock that evening, the door of Alex's cell opened and Conrad stood there, wearing a suit and tie. The smart clothes made his half-bald head, ruined face and red, twitching eye even uglier than usual. He reminded Alex of an expensive Guy Fawkes on bonfire night.

"You are invited to dinner," Conrad said.

"No thanks, Conrad," Alex replied. "I'm not hungry."

"The invitation is not one you may refuse." He tilted a hand to look at his watch. The hand had been inaccurately joined to the wrist. He had to move it a long way to see the watch face. "You have five minutes," he said. "You are expected to dress formally."

"I'm afraid I left my dinner jacket in England."

Conrad ignored him and closed the door.

Alex swung his legs off the bunk where he had been lying. He had been in the cell ever since his capture at the gate, vaguely wondering what was going to happen next. An invitation to dinner had been the last thing he'd expected. There had been no sign of Juan when he got back. Presumably the young guard had been reprimanded for his failure to watch over Alex and sent home. Or shot. Alex was beginning to realize that the people at the Casa de Oro meant business. He had no idea what Sarov had in mind for him this evening but he knew that the last time they had met, Alex had only just managed to escape with his life. He resembled the sixteen-year-old Vladimir, Sarov's lost son. Sarov must still have some fantasy about adopting him. Otherwise, he would now be dead.

He decided that, all in all, it would be wise to play along with this invitation to dinner. At the very least it might allow him to find out a little more about what was going on. Would the meal be filmed, he wondered? And if so, to what use would the film be put? Alex pulled a clean shirt and a pair of black Evisu trousers out of his case. He remembered that the mad headmaster, Dr Grief, had used hidden cameras at the Point Blanc academy to spy on the boys who were there. But this was different. The film that he had seen in the editing suite was being cut, pieced together, manipulated. It was going to be used for something. But what?

Conrad returned exactly five minutes later. Alex was ready for him. Once again he was escorted out of the slave house and up the steps to the main house. Inside, he heard the sound of classical music. He reached the courtyard and saw a trio – two elderly violinists and a plump lady with a cello – playing what sounded like Bach, the fountain tinkling softly behind them. There were about a dozen people gathered there, drinking champagne and eating canapés which were being carried round on silver trays by white-aproned waitresses. The four bodyguards were standing together in a tight, watchful circle. Another six men from the Russian delegation were chatting to the girls from the swimming pool, who glittered in sequins and jewellery.

The president himself was talking to Sarov, a glass in one hand and a huge cigar in the other. Sarov said something and he laughed out loud, smoke billowing from his lips. Sarov noticed Alex arrive and smiled.

"Ah, Alex! There you are! What will you have to drink?"

It seemed that the events of the afternoon had been forgotten. At least, they weren't to be mentioned again. Alex asked for a fresh orange juice and it was brought at once.

"I'm glad you're here, Alex," Sarov said. "I didn't want to start without you."

Alex remembered something Sarov had said at the swimming pool. Something about a surprise. He was beginning to have bad feelings about this dinner, but without knowing why.

The trio finished a piece of music and there was a light smattering of applause. Then a gong sounded and the guests moved into the dining room. This was the same room where Alex and Sarov had eaten breakfast, but it had been transformed for the banquet. The glasses were crystal, the plates brilliant white porcelain, the knives and forks polished till they gleamed. The tablecloth, also white, looked brand new. There were thirteen places for dinner – six on each side and one at the head. Alex noted the number with a further sense of unease. Thirteen for dinner. Unlucky.

Everyone took their places at the table. Sarov had placed himself at the head, with Alex on one side of him, Kiriyenko on the other. The doors opened and the waitresses came back in, this time with bowls brimming over with tiny black eggs which Alex recognized as caviar. Presumably Sarov had it directly imported from the Black Sea – it must have been worth many thousands of pounds. Russians traditionally drink vodka with caviar, and as the bowls were positioned around the table, the guests were each given a small tumbler filled to the brim.

Then Sarov stood up.

"My friends," he began. "I hope you will forgive me if I address you in English. There is unfortunately one guest at this table who has yet to learn our glorious language."

There were smiles around the table and a few heads nodded in Alex's direction. Alex looked down at the tablecloth, unsure how to respond.

"This is for me a night of great significance. What can I tell you about Boris Nikita Kiriyenko? He has been my closest and dearest friend for more than fifty years! It is strange to think that I can still remember him as a child who teased animals, who cried when there was a fight, and who never told the truth." Alex glanced at Kiriyenko. The president was frowning. Sarov was presumably joking, but the joke had failed to amuse his guest. "It is even harder to believe this is the same man who has been entrusted with the privilege, the sacred honour, of leading our great country in these difficult times. Well, Boris has come here for a holiday. I'm sure he needs one after so much hard work. And that is the toast that I wish to make tonight. To his holiday! I hope that it will be longer and more memorable than he ever expected."

There was a brief silence. Alex could see that the guests were puzzled. Perhaps they'd had difficulty following Sarov's English. But he suspected it was what he had said that had thrown them, not how he had said it. They had come expecting a good dinner, but Sarov seemed to be insulting the president of Russia!

"Alexei, my old friend!" the president said. Boris had decided that it *was* a joke. He smiled and continued in his thickly accented English. "Why do you not join us?" he asked.

"You know that I never drink spirits," Sarov replied. "And I hope you will agree that at fourteen, my son is a little too young for vodka."

"I drank my first vodka aged twelve!" the president muttered.

Somehow, Alex wasn't surprised.

Kiriyenko lifted his glass. "*Na zdarovie!*" he

said. They were about the only words of Russian that Alex understood. *Your health!*

"*Na zdarovie!*" Everyone round the table chorused the toast.

As one, they drank, throwing back the chilled vodka, as is traditional, in a single gulp.

Sarov turned to Alex. "Now it begins," he said quietly.

One of the bodyguards was the first to react. He had been reaching out to help himself to caviar when suddenly his hands jerked, dropping his fork and plate with a crash. Every head turned towards him. A second later, at the other end of the table, one of the other men threw himself forward, head-first, onto the table, his chair capsizing underneath him. As Alex watched, his eyes wide with horror, every person at the table began to react in the same way. One of them fell backwards, dragging the tablecloth with him, glasses and cutlery cascading into his lap. Several of them simply slumped where they sat. Another of the bodyguards managed to get to his feet and was scrabbling for a gun underneath his jacket, but then his eyes glazed and he collapsed. Boris Kiriyenko was the last to go. He was standing, swaying on his feet like a wounded bull. His fist was clenched as if he knew he had been betrayed and wanted to strike out at the man who had done it. Then he sat down heavily. His chair tilted and he was thrown onto the floor.

Sarov muttered a few words in Russian.

"What have you done?" Alex gasped. "Are they...?"

"They are unconscious, not dead," Sarov said. "They will, of course, have to be killed. But not yet."

"What are you planning?" Alex demanded. "What is it you're going to do?"

"We have a long journey," Sarov said. "I'll tell you on the way."

The entire compound was lit up. Men – guards and *macheteros* – were running everywhere. Alex was still dressed in the clothes he had worn for dinner. Sarov had changed into dark green military dress, this time without his medals. One of the black limousines was waiting. Conrad had driven up at the wheel of an army truck. As Alex watched, two more guards appeared at the main entrance of the Casa de Oro and began to walk down the wide steps. They were moving forward slowly, carrying something between them. The moment they appeared, everyone around them stopped.

It was a large silver chest about the size of a school trunk. Alex could just see that the top was flat metal, but that it had a number of switches and dials as well as some sort of slot device built into the side. Sarov watched while it was carried over and loaded into the truck. All the other men did the same, as if the two guards had just come out of a church and this was an an effigy of a saint. Alex shuddered. He knew exactly what he was looking at and didn't need the Geiger counter to confirm it.

This was the nuclear bomb.

"Alex?" Sarov was holding the car door open for him. Dazed, Alex got in. He knew that he had reached the end. Sarov had shown his hand and put into action a series of events from which there could be no going back. And yet even now, at this late stage, he had no idea what the general intended to do.

Sarov sat next to him. A driver got in and they moved off, Conrad following behind in the truck. At the very last moment, as they passed through the barrier, Sarov glanced back, very briefly. Alex saw the look in his eyes and knew that he had no intention ever to return. There were a hundred questions he wanted to ask, but he said nothing. This wasn't the time. Sarov was sitting quietly, his hands on his knees. But even he couldn't disguise the tension. Years of planning must have been building up to this.

They drove down darkened roads with just occasional flickers of light showing that the island was actually inhabited. No other cars came their way. After about ten minutes, they began to pass buildings. Looking out of the window, Alex saw men and women sitting in front of their houses, drinking rum, playing cards, smoking cigarettes or cigars beneath the night sky. They were on the outskirts of Santiago and suddenly they turned down a road that Alex recognized. He had taken it on the way in. They were going to the airport.

This time there was no security, no queues for passport control. Sarov didn't even have to enter the main terminal building. Two airport guards were waiting for him at a gate which was opened to allow him to drive straight onto the runway. The truck followed. Alex looked over the driver's shoulder and saw a plane, a Lear jet, parked on its own. They stopped.

"Out," Sarov said.

There was a breeze blowing across the airport runway, carrying with it the smell of aviation fuel. Alex stood on the tarmac, watching as the silver chest was loaded onto the plane, Conrad shouting instructions. He found it hard to believe that such an ordinary-looking thing could be capable of destruction on a massive scale. He remembered films he had seen. Flames and gale force winds rushing through whole cities, ripping them apart. Buildings crumbling. People turned to ashes in an instant. Cars and buses flicked like toys into oblivion. How could such a terrible bomb with so much power be so small? Conrad closed the cargo door himself. He turned to Sarov and nodded. Sarov gestured. Unwillingly, Alex walked forward and climbed the steps into the plane. Sarov was right behind him. Conrad and the two men who had been carrying the bomb followed. The door of the plane was closed and sealed.

Alex found himself in a luxurious compartment that was like no plane he had ever been in. There were only a dozen seats, each one upholstered in leather. The compartment was long and thickly carpeted, with a well stocked bar, a kitchen and, in front of the cockpit, a seventy centimetre plasma television screen. Alex didn't ask what film they would be showing. He chose a window seat – but then they were all window seats. Sarov sat across the aisle from him. Conrad was one seat behind Sarov. The two guards sat at the far end of the compartment. Alex wondered why they were making the journey. To keep an eye on him?

And what journey, exactly, were they making? Were they crossing into America or travelling across the Atlantic?

Sarov must have been reading his mind. "I will explain to you in a moment," he said. "As soon as we are in the air."

In fact, it was about fifteen minutes before the Lear jet took off down the runway and lifted effortlessly off the ground. The cabin lights dimmed for take-off but as soon as they had reached thirty thousand feet, they came back on. The guards got up and began to serve hot tea which had been brewing in an urn in the kitchen. Sarov allowed himself a brief smile. He pressed a button in the arm of his chair and swung round so that he now faced Alex.

"You may be wondering why I decided not to kill you," he began. "This afternoon, when I found you in the car ... I came so close. Conrad is still annoyed with me. He believes I am making a mistake. He does not understand me. But I will tell you why you are still alive, Alex. You are working for British intelligence. You are a spy. And you were only doing your job.

I admire that, and this is the reason why I have forgiven you. You are loyal to your country even as I am loyal to mine. My son Vladimir died for his country. I am proud that you were prepared to do the same for yours."

Alex took this in. "Where are we going?" he asked.

"We are going to Russia. To be precise, we are going to Murmansk, which is a port on the Kola Peninsula."

Murmansk! Alex tried to remember if he had heard the name before. It did seem familiar. Had he heard it in a news bulletin, or perhaps in a lesson at school? A port in Russia! But why would they be going there ... and carrying a nuclear bomb?

"You might like to know our flight path," Sarov continued. "We are crossing the Atlantic by the northern route. This involves flying over the Arctic Circle. In essence, we are taking a short cut, following the curvature of the earth. We will have to make two stops to refuel. One in Gander, in northern Canada. The other in the British Isles, in Edinburgh." Sarov must have seen the hopeful expression in Alex's eyes. He went on. "Yes. You will be home for an hour or two tomorrow. But please don't get any ideas. You will not be permitted to leave the plane."

"Will it really take so long to get there?" Alex asked.

"With the first stop and the time difference ... yes. We may also have to engage in some diplomatic pleasantries with both the Canadian and the British authorities. This is Kiriyenko's private plane. We have filed our flight plan with Euro Control and of course they recognized our serial number. They believe the president is onboard. I would imagine that the Canadian and the British governments might be keen to offer us hospitality."

"Who's flying the plane?"

"Kiriyenko's pilot. He is, however, loyal to me. A great many ordinary Russian people believe in me, Alex. They have seen the future ... my future. They prefer it to the version they have been offered by others."

"You still haven't told me what that future is. Why are we flying to Murmansk?"

"I will tell you now. And then we must both sleep. We have a long night ahead."

Sarov crossed his legs. There was a light directly above him and it beamed down, casting his eyes and mouth into shadow. He seemed at that moment both very old and very young. There was no expression in his face at all.

"Murmansk," he began, "is home to Russia's northern fleet of submarines. Or it was. It is now, quite simply, the world's biggest nuclear dustbin. The end of Russia as a world power has led to the rapid collapse of its army, air force and navy. I have already tried to explain to you what has happened to my country in the past thirty years. The way it has been allowed to fall apart, with poverty, crime and corruption sucking the people dry. Well, that process of decay can be seen most starkly in Murmansk.

"A fleet of nuclear submarines is moored there. I say 'moored' but I mean 'abandoned'. One of them, the *Lepse* is more than forty years old and contains six hundred and forty-two bundles of fuel rods. These submarines have been left to rot and they are falling apart. Nobody cares. Nobody can find the money to do anything about them. It is a well documented fact, Alex, that these old submarines represent the single biggest threat to the world today. There are one hundred of them! I am talking about one fifth of the world's nuclear fuel. One hundred ticking time bombs, waiting to go off. An accident waiting to happen. An accident I have decided to arrange."

Alex opened his mouth to break in, but Sarov

held up a hand for silence.

"Let me explain to you what would happen if just one of those submarines were to blow up," he continued. "First of all, a huge number of Russians in the Kola Peninsular and the north would be killed. Many more people would die in the neighbouring countries of Norway and Finland.

"Unusually for this time of year, the wind is blowing to the west, so the nuclear fallout would travel over Europe to your country. It is very possible that London would become uninhabitable. Over the years, thousands more people would fall ill and die slow, painful deaths."

"So why do it?" Alex shouted. "Why cause the explosion? What good will it do?"

"I am, if you like, giving the world a wake-up call," Sarov explained. "Tomorrow night I will land in Murmansk and I will place the bomb that you have seen amongst the submarines." He reached into his top pocket and took out a small plastic card. It had a magnetic stripe down one side like a credit card. "This is the key that will detonate the bomb," he said. "All the codes and information required are contained in the magnetic strip. All I have to do is insert the card into the bomb. At the time of the explosion itself,

I will be on my way south to Moscow, out of harm's way.

"The explosion will be felt in every country in the world. You can imagine the shock and the outrage that it will create. And nobody will know that it was caused by a bomb that was deliberately carried to Murmansk. They will believe that it was one of the submarines. The *Lepse*, perhaps, or one of the others. I've already said – it was an accident waiting to happen. And when it does happen, nobody will begin to suspect the truth."

"Yes they will!" Alex said. "The CIA know you bought uranium. They'll find out their agents are dead—"

"Nobody will believe the CIA. Nobody ever believes the CIA. And anyway, by the time they have assembled their evidence against me, it will be too late."

"I don't understand!" Alex exclaimed. "You've already said you'll kill thousands of your own people. What's the point?"

"You are young. You know nothing of my people. But listen to me, Alex, and I will explain. When this disaster happens, the whole world will unite in its condemnation of Russia. We will be hated. And the Russian people will be ashamed. If only we had been less careless, less stupid, less poor, less corrupt. If only we were still the super power we had once been. And it is at this moment that everyone – in Russia and in the world – will look to Boris Kiriyenko for leadership. The Russian president! And what will they see?"

"You made a film of him..." Alex muttered.

"We will release the film that shows him drunk beside the swimming pool. In his red shorts and flowered shirt. Playing with three half-naked women young enough to be his daughters! And we have interviewed him. We'll release that too."

"You've edited the interview!"

"Exactly." Sarov nodded, his eyes catching the light. "Our interviewer asked him about a train strike in Moscow and Kiriyenko, who was already half drunk, replied: 'This is my holiday. I'm too busy to deal with that.' We will change the question. 'What are you going to do about the accident in Murmansk?' And Kiriyenko will reply—"

"—'This is my holiday. I'm too busy to deal with that.'" Alex finished the sentence.

"The Russian people will see Kiriyenko for the weak, drunken imbecile that he is. They will very quickly blame him for the disaster at Murmansk – and with good reason. The northern fleet was once the pride of the whole nation. How could it have been allowed to become a rusting, leaking, lethal nuclear dump?"

The plane droned on. Conrad was listening intently to what Sarov was saying, his head balancing unevenly on his neck. The two guards at the back had gone to sleep.

"You said you would be in Moscow," Alex muttered.

"It will take less than twenty-four hours for the government to be swept out of power," Sarov replied. "There will be riots in the streets. Many Russians believe that life was better – much better – in the old days. They still believe in communism. Well, now their anger will be heard. It will be unstoppable. And I will be there to harness it, to use it to take power. I have followers who are waiting for it to happen. Before the nuclear cloud has settled, I will have total control of the country. And that is just the beginning, Alex. I will rebuild the Berlin Wall. There will be new wars. I will not rest until my kind of government, communist government, is the single dominant power in the world."

There was a long silence.

"You're prepared to kill millions of people to achieve this?" Alex asked.

Sarov shrugged. "Millions of people are dying

in Russia right now. They can't afford food. They can't afford medicine—"

"And what happens to me?"

"I've already answered that question, Alex. I don't believe it was a coincidence that you turned up the way you did. I believe it was meant to happen. I was never meant to do this on my own. You will be with me tomorrow and when the bomb is primed and ready, we will leave together. First Murmansk, then Moscow. Don't you see what I'm offering you? You are not just going to be my son. You are going to have power, Alex. You are going to be one of the most powerful people in the world."

The plane had already reached the coast of America and turned, beginning its journey north. Alex sank back in his seat, his head spinning. Absent-mindedly, he allowed his hand to slip into his trouser pocket. He had managed to bring one stick of the MI6 bubblegum with him. He also had the little figurine that was actually a stun grenade.

He closed his eyes and tried to work out what he was going to do.

SECURITY NIGHTMARE

Hours spent in a strange twilight that was neither night nor day. Trapped on the roof of the world, totally still yet hurtling ever further. Alex slept for the first part of the journey, knowing that he was tired and that he would need his strength. He had accepted what he had to do. Before, when they had been on Skeleton Key, a small part of him had been tempted to sit back and do nothing. After all, he had never asked to be there. All this had nothing to do with him.

But now everything had changed. He could see the nuclear blast in the Kola Peninsular. It was already there, in his imagination. Thousands of people would die instantly, tens of thousands later as the deadly radioactive particles spread over Europe. Britain would be one of the countries that would suffer. Alex had to stop it happening. He no longer had any choice.

It was going to be much more difficult this time. Sarov might have forgiven him for his failed escape attempt in the car but Alex knew he would no longer trust him. And he couldn't afford to make another mistake. If he was caught trying to escape a second time, there would be no reprieve, no mercy. In his heart, Alex seriously doubted that he would be able to slip past the Russian general or his twisted companion. Sarov was completely alert, as if he had been sitting there for ten minutes, not ten hours. Conrad was still watching him too. He was sitting quietly on the other side of the plane, a cat waiting for a mouse, his red eye blinking in the half light.

And yet...

Alex had the two gadgets Smithers had given him. And they were going to be landing in Britain! Just the thought of being in his own country, surrounded by people who spoke his language, gave Alex new strength. He had a plan and it would work. It had to.

He must have slept through the refuelling stop at Gander and several hours of the flight because the next thing he knew, it was light outside and the two guards were clearing away a breakfast of raw fruit and yoghurt that had been prepared in the Lear jet's miniature kitchen. He looked out of the window. All he could see was cloud.

Sarov noticed that he had woken up. "Alex! Are you hungry?"

"No, thank you."

"Still, you must have something to drink. It's very easy to dehydrate on these long journeys." He spoke a few words of Russian to one of the guards, who disappeared and came back with a glass of grapefruit juice. Alex hesitated before bringing it to his lips, remembering what had happened to Kiriyenko. Sarov smiled. "You don't need to worry," he said. "It's just grapefruit juice. No added ingredients."

Alex drank. The juice was cold and refreshing after his long sleep.

"We will be landing in Edinburgh in about thirty minutes," Sarov told him. "We're already in British airspace. How does it feel to be home?"

"If you'd like to drop me, I can get a train to London."

Sarov shook his head. "I'm afraid not."

A few minutes later they began their descent. The pilot had been in radio communication with the airport and had confirmed that this was a routine refuelling stop. He would not be dropping or picking up any passengers and so needed no operating permit. Everything had been cleared with the airport authorities, making this touchdown as simple as a car pulling into a local garage. And despite Sarov's fears, the British government had not invited the supposed VIP passengers for a diplomatic breakfast in Edinburgh!

The plane broke through the cloud and, with his face pressed against the window, Alex suddenly saw countryside with miniature houses and cars dotted around it. The brilliant sunshine of the Caribbean had been replaced by the grey light and uncertain weather of a British summer's day. He felt a sense of relief. He was back! But at the same time, he knew Sarov would never allow him off the plane. In a way, it would have been less cruel if they had refuelled in Greenland or Norway. He was being given one last look at his own country. The next time he saw it, it would have been poisoned for generations to come. Alex reached into his pocket. His hand closed around the figurine of Michael Owen. The time was getting close...

The seat-belt signs came on. A moment later, Alex felt the pressure in his ears as they dropped out of the sky. He saw a bridge, somehow delicate from this height, spanning a great stretch of water. The Forth Road Bridge ... it had to be. And there was Edinburgh, over in the west, its castle dominating the skyline. The airport came rushing up. He caught a glimpse of a bright, modern terminal, of waiting planes sitting on the apron surrounded by vans and trolleys. There was a bump as the wheels made contact with the runway and then the roar of the engines in reverse thrust. The plane slowed. They had landed.

Guided by the control tower, the Lear jet made its way to the end of the runway and into an area known as the fuel farm, far away from the main terminal. Alex gazed out of the window with a sinking feeling as the public buildings slid away behind him. For every second that they travelled, he would have further to run to raise the alarm – always assuming that he did even manage to get off the plane. The Michael Owen figure was in his hand now. What had Smithers told him? Twist the head twice one way and once the other to arm it. Wait ten seconds, then drop it and run. The confined space of an aircraft cabin seemed the perfect place to try it out. The only question was, how was Alex going to stop it knocking himself out too?

They came to a halt. Almost at once, a fuel truck

began to drive towards them. Sarov had obviously prepared everything well in advance. There was a car following the truck and, looking out of the window, Alex saw that steps were being led up to the Lear jet's door. That was interesting. It seemed that somebody wanted to come onboard.

Sarov was watching him. "You will not speak, Alex," he said. "Not one single word. Before you even think of opening your mouth, I suggest you look behind you."

Conrad had moved into the seat directly behind Alex. He had a newspaper balanced on his lap. As Alex turned, he lifted it to reveal a large black pistol with a silencer, pointing directly at him.

"Nobody will hear anything," Sarov said. "If Conrad even thinks you are about to try something, he will fire. The bullet will pass through the seat and into your spine. Death will be instant but it will appear that you have simply fallen asleep."

Alex knew that it wouldn't be as easy as that. A person being shot in the back did not look like a person falling asleep. Sarov was taking huge risks. But this whole business was a huge risk. The stakes couldn't be higher. Alex had no doubt that if he tried to tell anyone what was happening he would be killed immediately.

The door of the plane opened and a ginger-haired man in blue overalls entered, carrying a sheaf of papers. Sarov rose to greet him. "Do you speak English?" the man asked in a Scottish accent.

"Yes."

"I have some papers here for you to sign."

Alex turned his head slightly. The man saw him and nodded. Alex nodded back. He could almost feel Conrad pressing the back of his seat with the gun. He said nothing. And then it was over. Sarov had signed the papers and returned the man's pen.

"Here's a receipt for you," the man said, handing Sarov a sheet. "And we'll have you back in the air in no time at all."

"Thank you." Sarov nodded.

"Are you going to come out and stretch your legs? It's a pleasant day here in Edinburgh. We can offer you some tea and shortbread if you want to come to the office."

"No, thank you. We're all a little tired. We'll stay where we are."

"OK. If you're absolutely sure, I'll get rid of the steps..."

They were going to take away the steps – and

as soon as they were gone, Sarov would seal the door! Alex had only seconds in which to act. He waited until the man had left the cabin, then stood up. His hands were in front of him, the Michael Owen figure lying concealed in his palm.

"Sit down!" Conrad hissed.

"It's all right, Conrad," Alex said. "I'm not going anywhere. I'm just stretching my legs."

Sarov had sat down again. He was examining the paperwork the man had given him. Alex strolled past him. His mouth was dry and he was glad that the sensor that had been used at the gate of the Casa de Oro wasn't on the plane. If it had been turned on him now, his heartbeat would have been deafening. This was his last chance. Alex carefully measured out each step. If he had been walking towards his own scaffold, he couldn't have been more tense.

"Where are you going, Alex?" Sarov asked.

Alex turned Michael Owen's head twice.

"I'm not going anywhere."

"What's that you've got in your hands?"

Alex hesitated. But if he tried to pretend he had nothing, Sarov would become even more suspicious than he already was. He held up the figurine. "It's my lucky mascot," he said. "Michael Owen."

He took another step forward. He gave the player's head another turn back.

Ten ... nine ... eight ... seven...

"Sit down, Alex," Sarov said.

"I've got a headache," Alex said. "I just want some fresh air."

"You are not to leave the plane."

"I'm not going anywhere, General."

But Alex had already reached the door and felt the fresh Scottish breeze on his face. A tow-truck was pulling the steps away. He watched as a gap opened up between them and the door.

Four ... three ... two...

"Alex! Return to your seat!"

Alex dropped the figurine and threw himself forward.

Conrad leapt up like an angry snake, the gun in his hand.

The figurine exploded.

Alex felt the blast behind him. There was a flash of light and a bang that sounded massively loud, although no windows broke and there was no fire or smoke. His ears rang and for a moment he couldn't see. But he was outside the plane. He had been outside the plane when the stun grenade went off. The steps were still moving away, disappearing in front of him. He was going to miss them! The asphalt surface of the fuel farm apron was five metres below. If he fell that distance, he would break a leg. He might even be killed. But he had made his move just in time. He landed flat on his stomach on the top of the staircase with his legs dangling in the air. Quickly he pulled himself to his feet. The man with the ginger hair was staring at him, astonished. Alex ran down the still-moving steps. As his feet came into contact with the ground, he felt a thrill of triumph. He was home. And it seemed that the stun grenade had done its job. There was no movement on the plane. Nobody was firing at him.

"What the hell do you think you're doing?" the man demanded.

Alex ignored him. This wasn't the right person to be talking to – and he needed to put as much distance as he could between himself and the plane. Smithers had said that the grenade would only incapacitate the enemy for a few minutes. Sarov and Conrad would wake up soon. And they would waste no time in coming after him.

He ran. Out of the corner of his eye, he saw the man snatch a radio out of his pocket and talk into it – but that didn't matter. There were other men around the plane, about to start refuelling. They must surely have heard the explosion. Even if

Alex was recaptured, the plane wouldn't be allowed to leave.

But he had no intention of being recaptured. He had already noticed a row of administrative buildings on the perimeter of the airfield and he made for them, the breath rasping in his throat. He reached a door and pulled at it. It was locked! He looked through the window. There was a hallway on the other side and a public telephone, but for some reason the building was closed. For a moment he was tempted to smash the glass – but that would take too long. Cursing quietly, he left the door and ran the twenty metres to the next building.

This one was open. He found himself in a corridor with storerooms and offices on either side. There didn't seem to be anyone about. Now all he needed was a phone. He tried a door. It led into a room full of shelves with a photocopier and stationery supplies. The next door was locked. Alex was getting increasingly desperate. He tried another door and this time he was lucky. It was an office with a desk and, on the desk, a telephone. There was nobody inside. He ran in and snatched it up.

But it was only now he realized that he had no idea what number to ring. The mobile that

Smithers had given him had been equipped with a hot key – a direct link to MI6. But nobody had ever given him a direct number. What was he to do? Dial the operator and ask for military intelligence? They would think he was mad.

He didn't have any time to waste. Sarov might already have recovered. Even now he might be on his way. The office had a window but it looked out the back, so there was no sign of the plane or the runway. Alex made a decision and dialled 999.

The line rang twice before it was answered.

It was a woman's voice. "You have rung the emergency services. Which service do you require?"

"Police," Alex said.

"Connecting you now..."

He heard the ring tone.

And then a hand came down onto the telephone, cutting him off. Alex swung round, breathless, expecting to see Sarov in front of him – or worse still, Conrad with the gun.

But it wasn't either of them. It was an airport security guard who had walked into the office while Alex was making his call. He was about fifty years old with greying hair and a chin that had sunk into his neck. His stomach bulged over his belt and his trousers stopped about two centimetres short of his ankles. The man had a radio attached to his jacket. His name – George Prescott – was written on a badge on his top pocket. He was looming over Alex with a stern look on his face and, with a sinking heart, Alex recognized a real security nightmare: a man with the self-important smugness of the traffic warden, the car park attendant, any petty official.

"What are you doing here, laddie?" Prescott demanded.

"I need to make a telephone call," Alex said.

"I can see that. But this isn't a public telephone. This isn't even a public office. This is a secure complex. You shouldn't be in here."

"No, you don't understand. This is an emergency!"

"Oh yes? And what sort of emergency do you mean?" Prescott obviously didn't believe him.

"I can't explain. Just let me make the call."

The security guard smiled. He was enjoying himself. He spent five days a week plodding from one office to another, checking doors and turning off lights. It was good to have someone he could boss about. "You're not making any calls until you tell me what you're doing here!" he said. "This is a private office." His eyes narrowed.

"Have you opened any drawers? Have you taken anything?"

Alex's nerves were screaming but he forced himself to remain calm. "I haven't taken anything, Mr Prescott," he said. "I just got off a plane that landed a few minutes ago—"

"What plane?"

"A private plane."

"Have you got a passport?"

"No."

"That's a very serious matter. You can't enter the country without a passport."

"My passport is on the plane!"

"Then I'll escort you back and we'll get it."

"No!" Alex could feel the seconds racing by. What could he say to this man that would persuade him to let him make the phone call? His mind was in a whirl and suddenly, for the first time in his life, he found himself blurting out the truth. "Listen," he said. "I know this is hard to believe, but I work for the government. The British government. If you let me call them, they'll prove it to you. I'm a spy—"

"A spy?" Prescott's face broke into a smile. But there was no humour in it at all. "How old are you?"

"Fourteen."

"A fourteen-year-old spy? I think you've been

watching too much television, laddie."

"It's true!"

"I don't think so."

"Listen to me, please. A man has just tried to kill me. He's on a plane on the runway and unless you let me make this call, a lot of people are going to die."

"What?"

"He's got a nuclear bomb, for God's sake!"

That was a mistake. Prescott bristled. "I'll ask you not to take the name of the Lord in vain, if you don't mind." He came to a decision. "I don't know how you got here or what you're playing at, but you're coming with me to security and pass-port control in the main terminal." He reached out for Alex. "Come along now! I've had enough of your nonsense."

"It isn't nonsense. There's a man called Sarov. He's carrying a nuclear bomb. He's planning to detonate it in Murmansk. I'm the only one who can stop him. Please, Mr Prescott. Just let me phone the police. It'll only take me twenty sec-onds and you can stand here and watch me. Let me talk to them and afterwards you can take me wherever you like."

But the security guard wouldn't budge. "You're not making any calls and you're coming with me now," he said.

Alex made up his mind. He had tried pleading and he had tried telling the truth. Neither had succeeded, so he would just have to take the security guard out. Prescott moved round the desk, getting closer to him. Alex tensed himself, balancing on the balls of his feet, his fists ready. He knew that the man was only doing his job and he didn't want to hurt him but there was no other way.

And then the door opened.

"There you are, Alex! I was worried about you..."

It was Sarov.

Conrad was with him. Both of them looked ill – their skin white and eyes not quite focused. There was no expression on either man's face.

"Who are you?" Prescott demanded.

"I'm Alex's father," Sarov replied. "Isn't that right, Alex?"

Alex hesitated. He realized he was still in combat position, about to strike out. Slowly, he lowered his arms. He knew it was over and tasted the bitterness of defeat. There was nothing he could do. If he argued in front of Prescott, Sarov would simply kill both of them. If he tried to fight, the result would be just the same. Alex had just one hope left. If he walked out of here with Sarov and Conrad and the security guard was still alive, there was just a chance that he might tell his story to someone who would report it to MI6. It would certainly be too late for Alex. But the world might still be saved.

"Isn't that right, Alex?" Sarov was waiting for an answer.

"Yes," Alex said. "Hello, Dad."

"So what's all this business about bombs and spies?" Prescott asked.

Alex inwardly groaned. Why couldn't the man keep his mouth shut?

"Is that what Alex has been telling you?" Sarov asked.

"Aye. That and a whole lot more besides."

"Has he made a telephone call?"

"No." Prescott puffed himself up. "The wee rascal was helping himself to the phone when I came in. But I soon put a stop to that."

Sarov nodded slowly. He was pleased. "Well ... he does have a vivid imagination," he explained. "Alex has not been well lately. He has mental problems. Sometimes he finds it hard to distinguish between fantasy and reality."

"How did he get in here?" Prescott demanded.

"He must have slipped out of the plane when nobody was watching. He has, of course, no permission to be on British soil."

"Is he British?"

"No." Sarov took hold of Alex's arm. "And now we must return to the plane. We still have a long journey ahead of us."

"Wait a minute!" The guard wasn't going to let them off that easily. "I'm sorry, sir, but your son was strictly off-limits. And for that matter, so are you. You can't just go wandering around Edinburgh airport like this! I'm going to have to report this."

"I quite understand." Sarov didn't seem at all perturbed. "I must get the boy back on the plane. But I will leave you with my assistant, who will give you all the details you require. If necessary, he will accompany you to your superior's office. And I have to thank you for preventing my son from making a telephone call, Mr Prescott. That would have been most embarrassing for us all."

Without waiting for a reply, Sarov turned and, still holding Alex's arm, led him out of the room.

An hour later, the Lear jet took off on the last leg of its journey. Alex was sitting in the same seat as before but now he was handcuffed to it. Sarov hadn't hurt him and no longer seemed even aware that he was on the plane. In a way, that was the most frightening thing about him. Alex had expected anger, violence, perhaps even a sudden death at the hands of Conrad. But Sarov had done nothing. From the moment that Alex had been escorted back onto the plane, the Russian hadn't so much as looked at him. There had, of course, been problems. The explosion on the plane and Alex's leap out of it had raised all sorts of questions. The pilot had been in constant communication with the control tower. The sound of the explosion had been a faulty microwave oven, he'd explained. As for the boy? General Alexei Sarov, on the staff of the Russian president, was travelling with a nephew. The boy had high spirits. Very stupid, but everything was under control...

If this had been an ordinary private jet, the police would have been called. But it was registered to Boris Kiriyenko. It had diplomatic immunity. All in all, the authorities agreed, it would be easier to turn a blind eye and let it go.

George Prescott's body was discovered four hours later. He was sitting, slumped, in a stationery cupboard. There was a look of surprise on his face and a single, round bullet wound between his eyes.

By then, the Lear was in Russian airspace. Even as the alarm was raised and the police were finally called, the cabin lights were dimmed as the jet curved over the Kola Peninsula preparing for its final descent.

THE END OF THE WORLD

Airports are the same all over the world, but the one at Murmansk had managed to achieve a new level of ugliness. It had been built in the middle of nowhere so that, from the air, it looked like a mistake. At ground level, it offered just one low-rise terminal built out of glass and tired, grey cement, with eight white letters mounted on the roof.

МУРМАНСК

Alex recognized the Russian spelling. Murmansk. A city with thousands of people. He wondered how many of them would be alive in twelve hours' time.

Now handcuffed to one of the two guards who had flown with them all the way from Skeleton Key, he was led across an empty runway. It had rained recently. The asphalt was wet and greasy, with pools of dirty water all around. There were no other planes in sight. In fact, the airport didn't seem to be in use at all. A few lights burned, dull yellow, behind the glass. But there were no people. The single arrivals door was locked and chained as if the airport had given up all hope of anyone ever actually coming there.

They were expected. Three army trucks and a mud-streaked saloon car were waiting. A row of men stood to attention, dressed in khaki uniforms with black belts and boots almost like wellingtons rising to their calves. Each one of them carried a machine-gun on a strap across his chest. Their commander, wearing the same uniform as Sarov, stepped forward and saluted. He and Sarov shook hands, then embraced. They spoke for a few minutes. Then the commander snapped an order. Two of his men ran to the plane and began to unload the silver chest that was Sarov's nuclear bomb. Alex watched as it was taken out of the back and loaded into one of the trucks. The soldiers were well disciplined. Here was enough power to destroy a continent, but not one head turned as it was carried past.

With the bomb in place, the soldiers swivelled round and, marching in time, approached the two remaining trucks and climbed in. His hands cuffed together now, Alex was bundled into the front seat of one, next to the driver. Nobody looked at him. Nobody seemed too curious about who he was. Sarov must have radioed ahead and warned them that he would be there. He examined the man driving the truck. He was tough and clean-shaven with clear blue eyes. There was no expression on his face. A professional soldier. Alex turned and looked out of the window in time to see Sarov and Conrad getting into the car.

They set off. There really was nothing outside the airport, just a flat, empty landscape where even the trees managed to be stunted and dull. Alex shivered and tried to cross his hands to rub warmth into his shoulders. There was a clink from the handcuffs and the driver glanced at him angrily.

They drove for about forty minutes down a road pitted with holes. A few buildings, modern and characterless, crept up on them and suddenly they were in Murmansk itself. Was it night or day? The sky was still light but the streetlamps were on. There were people on the pavements but they didn't seem to be going anywhere, just drifting along like sleepwalkers. Nobody looked at them as they followed a single road, four lanes wide. This was a boulevard in the centre of the city.

It was absolutely straight and seemed to go nowhere, with blank, uninteresting buildings on either side. Murmansk was made up of row after row of almost identical apartment blocks like so many match boxes. There didn't seem to be any cinemas, restaurants, shops – anything that would make life worth living.

There were no suburbs. The city just stopped and suddenly they were driving through empty tundra, heading for a horizon that had nothing at all to offer. They were fourteen hundred kilometres from the North Pole and there was nothing here. People with no life and a sun without a shred of warmth. Alex thought of the journey he had made. From Wimbledon to Cornwall. Then London, Miami and Skeleton Key. And finally here. Was it to be *finally*? What a horrible place to finish his life. He really had come to the end of the world.

There were no other cars on the road and no street signs. Alex stopped even trying to see where they were going. After another thirty minutes they began to slow down, then turned off. There was a crunching sound under the wheels as they left the asphalt surface and continued along gravel. Was this where the Russians kept their submarines? He could only see a chicken wire fence and a dilapidated wooden kiosk trying to pass as a sentry box.

They stopped in front of a red and white barrier. A man appeared, dressed in dark blue with a loose, flapping overcoat and, showing underneath it, a tunic and a striped T-shirt. He was a Russian sailor. He couldn't have been more than twenty years old and he looked confused. He ran over to the car and said something in Russian.

Conrad shot him. Alex saw the hand come out of the window and the flash of the gun, but it all happened so quickly that he could hardly believe it had happened at all. The young Russian was thrown backwards. Conrad fired a second time. There was another sailor in the sentry box – Alex hadn't even noticed him – and he shouted out, crumpling backwards. Nobody had spoken a word. Two soldiers climbed out of the front truck and went over to the barrier blocking the entrance. Was this really the entrance to a submarine base? Alex had seen more sophisticated security in a supermarket carpark. The soldiers simply lifted the barrier. The convoy moved on.

They followed a twisting, bumpy track down a hill and there, at last, was the sea. The first thing Alex saw was a fleet of ice-breakers, moored about eight hundred metres away, huge iron blocks sitting silently, impossibly on the sea. It seemed against the laws of nature that such monstrous things could float. There were no lights onboard, no movement at all. On the other side of the water, another grim stretch of coastline rose up, streaked with white; though whether this was salt or some sort of permanent snow, Alex couldn't say.

The trucks bounced down and suddenly they were in a harbour, surrounded by cranes, gantries, warehouses and sheds. It was a devil's playground of twisted steel and cement, of hooks and chains, pulleys and cables, drums, wooden pallets and huge steel containers. Rusting ships sat in the water or stood on dry land, suspended on a network of stilts. Cars, lorries and tractors, some obviously derelict, stood idle at the water's edge. There was a row of long wooden cabins to one side, each one numbered in yellow and grey paint. They reminded Alex of buildings he'd seen in old World War Two movies, in prisoner of war camps. Could this be where the other sailors slept? If so, they must all be in bed. The harbour was deserted. Nothing moved.

They stopped and Alex felt the truck rock as the soldiers poured out behind him. A moment later he saw them, their machine-guns raised, and wondered if he was meant to follow them. But the driver shook his head, gesturing at him to stay where he was. Alex watched the men fan out across the compound, moving quickly as they made for the cabins. There was no sign of Sarov. He must still be in the car, which was parked round the other side.

A long pause. Then someone gave a signal. There was the smash of wood, a door being forced open, then the concentrated chatter of machine-gun fire. Somebody shouted. An electric bell began to ring, the sound all too small and ineffective. Three half-dressed men appeared round the side of the cabins and sprinted forward, trying to find shelter among the containers. More gunfire. Alex saw two of them go down, followed by the third, his hands scrabbling at the air as he was hit in the back. There was a single shot from a window. One man was trying to fight back. A grenade curved through the air and onto the roof of the building. There was an explosion and half the wall blew out, turned into matchsticks. The next time Alex looked, the window and presumably the man behind it had been destroyed.

The attack had come without any warning at all. Sarov's men had been well armed and prepared. There had only been a handful of sailors at the yard and they had all been asleep. It was over very quickly. The ringing stopped. Smoke curled out of the damaged building. A figure floated past, face down in the water. The harbour had been taken. Sarov was in total command.

The driver got out of the truck, went quickly round the front and opened the door for Alex. He climbed down awkwardly, his hands still chained together. Sarov's men had moved into the second phase of the operation. Alex saw bodies being carried out of sight. One of the other trucks reversed, moving closer to the water's edge. The commander from the airport called out an order and the soldiers scattered, taking up positions that they must have worked out months before. It seemed unlikely that anybody would have had time to raise the alarm, but if anyone approached the yard from Murmansk, they would find it defended. Sarov was standing to one side with Conrad beside him. He was looking at something. Alex followed his eyes.

And there were the submarines!

Alex gasped. Here was what this whole thing had been about! There were just four of them, bloated metal beasts that lay half-submerged in the sea, secured by ropes as thick as a man's arm. Each one was the size of an office building turned on its side. The submarines had no markings whatsoever and no flags. They seemed to be coated in black oil or tar. Their conning towers, set well back, were closed and solid. Alex shivered.

He'd never thought that a machine could actually emanate evil, but these did. They were as dark and as cold as the water that lapped about them. They looked just like the bombs that they had become.

Three of the submarines were in a line, moored against the side of the harbour. The fourth was in a bay of its own, a little way out. Alex noticed a crane at the end of a quay, right next to the water. Years ago it might have been painted yellow but most of the colour had flaked off. The control cabin was only about ten metres above the ground with a ladder reaching up to it. The arm of the crane slanted up, then bent down, mimicking the neck and head of a bird. This was a crane with no hook. Instead there was a metal disc like an oversized bath plug dangling underneath the arm, connected to it by a chain and a series of electric cables.

Conrad shouted something and the driver led Alex over to a solid handrail on the edge of the quay. It had obviously been placed there to stop anyone falling in and it was securely bolted to the ground. The driver unlocked one of Alex's hands then pulled with the chain, leading him like a dog. He walked him over to the handrail and cuffed him to it. Alex was left standing on his own in the middle of everything. He jerked at the chain but it was useless. He wasn't going anywhere.

Alex could only stand and watch as two of the soldiers lifted the bomb out of the truck as carefully as they could. He saw the strain in their faces as they set it on the ground right next to the edge of the quay and only a few metres from the crane. Sarov walked over, Conrad limping along next to him. Conrad looked at Alex and one corner of his mouth twitched into a smile.

Sarov reached into his jacket pocket and took out the plastic card he had shown Alex on the plane. He held it for a moment, then fed it into the slot on the side of the nuclear bomb. At once, the silver chest came to life. A series of red lights began to blink on a panel. Alex saw a line of digits on a liquid crystal display. Hours, minutes and seconds. They were already counting down. The magnetic stripe on the card had activated the bomb. Somewhere inside the chest, electronic wheels were turning. The detonation sequence had begun.

Then Sarov came over to Alex.

He stood there, examining him as if for the first and last time. As ever, his face gave nothing away, but Alex detected something in the man's eyes. Sarov would have denied it. He would have been angered if anyone had suggested it. But the sadness was there. It was plain to see.

"And so we come to the end," he said. "You are standing in the Nuclear Submarine Repair Shipyard of Murmansk. You may be interested to know that the soldiers we met at the airport have all served with me in the past and are loyal to me still. The entire compound is now under my control and as you have seen, the nuclear bomb is primed. I'm afraid I cannot stay with you any longer. I have to return to the airport to ensure that everything is ready for our flight to Moscow. I will leave Conrad to place the bomb in position on the submarine, directly over the nuclear reactor that is still there inside. It is possible that the detonator in the bomb will also trigger the reactor, doubling or trebling the force of the explosion. This will mean very little to you, as you will be vaporized instantly – before your brain has time even to work out what has happened. Conrad is very disappointed. He had hoped I would allow him to kill you himself."

Alex said nothing.

"I am so sorry, Alex, that in the end you were so much more stupid than I had thought, although perhaps I should have expected it. A Western child, brought up and educated in Britain ... a country that is itself only a shadow of what it once was. Why couldn't you see what I was offering you? Why couldn't you accept your place in the new world? You could have been my son. You chose to be my enemy. And this is where it has brought you."

There was another, long silence. Sarov reached out and gently stroked Alex's cheek. He looked into the boy's eyes one last time. Then he turned on his heel and walked away. Alex watched him get into his car and drive off.

The other soldiers were a distance away, still in their places around the site. But here at the centre, with the crane, the submarines and the nuclear bomb, Alex and Conrad were on their own. It was as if they had the whole harbour to themselves.

Conrad stepped forward and stopped very close to Alex. "I have a job to do," he rasped. "But then we will have a little time together. Strange though it is, Sarov still cares about you. He told me to leave you alone. But I think, this time, I must disobey the general. You are mine! And I intend to make you suffer..."

"Just talking to you makes me suffer," Alex said.

Conrad ignored him. He went over to the crane and climbed the short ladder into the cabin. Alex saw him start up the controls and a moment later the metal disc swung round so that it was over the bomb, then began to descend. Conrad handled the crane expertly. The disc fell quickly, stopped, then gently came into contact with the surface of the chest. Alex heard a loud click and a moment later the chest suddenly swayed and left the ground. Now he understood. The metal disc was a powerful electromagnet. Conrad was operating a magnetic hoist, using it to carry the bomb across the water and deposit it on the submarine. The whole operation would take him about three minutes. Then he would come for Alex.

Alex had run out of time. He had to act now.

The stick of bubblegum that Smithers had given him was in his right pocket. Only his left hand was free and it took him a few precious seconds to get it out, unwrap it and shove it into his mouth. He wondered what Conrad would think if he had seen him. Certainly Sarov wouldn't have been amused. A Western boy about to face death and all he could think about was gum!

Alex chewed. Smithers had managed to get one part of the formula right. The gum did indeed taste of strawberries. He wondered how long he should leave it in his mouth. His saliva was meant to activate it, but how much saliva did it need? He chewed until the gum felt soft and manageable and the strawberry taste had faded away. Then he spat it into his hand and quickly pressed it into the handcuff, forcing it into the lock.

The silver chest had travelled all the way across the water. Alex saw it swinging gently over the submarine. Inside the control cabin, Conrad leaned forward. Slowly he lowered the chest until it landed on the metal surface. The wires and chains attached to the hoist sagged, then straightened again. The hoist began to move back towards the quay. But it had left the bomb behind.

Something was definitely happening inside the handcuffs. Alex heard a very faint hissing. The pink gum was expanding. It was oozing back out of the lock and there was much more gum coming out than he had put in. There was a sudden crack. The metal had shattered. Alex felt a painful sting as a piece of broken metal cut into his wrist. But then the handcuffs fell open. He was free!

Conrad had seen what had happened. He was already climbing out of the crane. He hadn't turned off the controls and the magnet was still coming back on its own, just a few metres above the water. The bomb was out of reach on the other side. Even as Alex looked around for a weapon, Conrad reached the bottom of the ladder and rushed towards him. Suddenly they were face to face.

Conrad smiled. The smile tugged at the one side of his face that could move. The other side, with the bald scalp above it, remained still. Alex could see at once that, despite all his terrible injuries, Conrad was utterly confident. A moment later, he knew why. Fired by hatred, Conrad moved with surprising speed. He was standing in combat stance one moment, a blur the next. Alex felt a foot kick him in the chest. The world spun and he was thrown to the ground, winded and bruised. Meanwhile, Conrad had landed lightly on his feet. He wasn't even out of breath.

Painfully, Alex picked himself up. Conrad walked towards him and lashed out a second time. His foot missed by a centimetre as Alex dived back to the ground, rolling over and over to the water's edge. A hand reached out and grabbed hold of his shirt. Alex saw the dreadful stitch-marks where the hand had been sewn back onto the wrist. He was dragged to his feet. Conrad slapped him with tremendous force. Alex tasted blood. The hand released him. He stood, swaying, trying to find some sort of defence.

But he had none. For all his strength and skill, Conrad had beaten him. And now he was coming in for the kill. Alex saw it in his face...

And then, out of nowhere, came a sudden clanging. The alarm bell had started up again. There was a burst of gunfire and, seconds later, an explosion. Someone had thrown another grenade. Conrad stopped dead in his tracks, his head twisting round. There was more gunfire. Impossible though it was, it seemed that the harbour was under attack.

With new strength, Alex ran forward. He had seen a metal rod lying on the ground amongst all the other debris. His hands closed around it and he swept it up, grateful to have something that felt like a weapon in his hands. Conrad turned to face him. The shooting had intensified. Now it seemed to be coming from two directions as Sarov's men defended themselves against an enemy that had come from nowhere. There was a screech of tyres, and in the far distance Alex saw a jeep come smashing through one of the chicken wire fences. It skidded to a halt and three men jumped out and took cover. They were all dressed in blue. What was going on here? The Russian navy against the Russian army? And who, exactly, had raised the alarm?

But even if Sarov's plans had been revealed, even if a rescue operation had somehow been put in place, Alex was still in grave danger. Conrad was on the balls of his feet, looking to find a way past the metal rod. And what about the nuclear bomb? Alex didn't know if Sarov had primed it to go off in five hours or five minutes. Knowing how mad he was, it could have been either.

Conrad leapt forward. Alex lunged with the metal

pole and felt it ram into the man's shoulder. But his smile of satisfaction vanished as Conrad grabbed hold of the rod with both hands. He had allowed Alex to hit him simply because that would bring the rod within his reach. Alex pulled back, but Conrad was much too strong for him. He felt the metal being torn out of his hands, cutting into his palms. Alex let go of the rod, then cried out as Conrad swung it viciously like a scythe. The metal slammed into the side of Alex's leg and he was down again, on his back, unable to move.

More gunfire. Although his vision was dimmed, Alex saw two more grenades arc through the air. They landed next to one of the ships and exploded, a huge fireball of flame. Two of Sarov's men were lifted into the air. Two or even three machine-guns began to chatter simultaneously. There were screams. More flames.

Conrad stood over him.

He seemed to have forgotten what was happening in the shipyard. Or perhaps he didn't care. He pulled up one sleeve, then the other. Finally he dropped down so that he was sitting on Alex's chest, one knee on either side. His hands closed around Alex's throat.

Gently, enjoying what he was doing, he began to squeeze.

Alex felt himself being slowly strangled. He couldn't breathe. There were already black spots in front of his eyes. But he had seen something that Conrad hadn't. It was slowly making its way back towards them, crossing the water. The magnetic disc.

Conrad had left the controls on in the cabin in his haste to get over to Alex. Was it possible...? Alex remembered what Sarov had told him about his assistant. He had metal pins all over his body. There were metal wires in his jaw and a metal plate in his head...

The magnet was almost over them, blotting out the sky. Alex couldn't breathe. Conrad's hands were tight around his throat. He had only seconds left.

With the last of his strength, he suddenly lashed out with both his fists, at the same time jerking his body up. Conrad was taken by surprise. He started back, his hands loosening. The magnet was right above him. Alex saw the shock in his face as all the metal plates, pins and wires in his body entered the magnetic field. Conrad yelled and disappeared, plucked into the air by invisible hands. His back smashed into the disc with a terrible snapping sound. At once he went still, attached to the disc by his shoulders, his arms and legs hanging down.

The crane continued moving, carrying the limp body in a gentle curve over the quay.

Alex gasped for breath. The world swam back into focus. "What an attractive man," he muttered.

Slowly, he pulled himself to his feet, then staggered over to the handrail where he had been chained. He propped himself against it, no longer able to stand without its support. There was a burst of gunfire, longer and more powerful than any that had gone before. A helicopter had appeared, flying in low over the sea. He saw an airman sitting in the open doorway, his legs dangling, a huge gun cradled in his lap. One of Sarov's trucks was blown off its wheels, twisted over twice and exploded in flames.

The bomb...

Alex could work out what was happening here later. Nobody would be safe until the bomb was defused. His throat was still burning. It took all his strength to draw breath. But now he ran forward and climbed into the crane. He had operated a crane before. He knew it couldn't be too difficult. He reached out and took the controls. At the same moment, one of Sarov's men fired at him. The bullet clanged against the metal casing of the cabin. Alex ducked instinctively and pulled a lever.

The magnetic disc stopped and swung in the

air with Conrad stuck beneath it like a broken doll. Alex pushed forward and it began to drop down into the sea. No! That wasn't what he wanted. He pulled the lever back and it stopped abruptly. How did you turn off the magnet? Alex looked around him and saw a switch. He pressed it. A light came on over his head. Wrong switch! There was a button set in the control stick he was holding and he tried that. At once, Conrad fell free. He plunged into the grey, freezing water and sank immediately. With all the metal inside him, Alex thought, it was hardly surprising.

He pulled the control stick towards him and the magnet rose again. A soldier ran across the quay towards him. There was a burst of fire from the helicopter and the man fell down and lay still. Now ... concentrate! Alex tried a second lever and this time the magnet began its return journey over to the submarine. It seemed to take for ever. Alex was only partly aware of the battle still raging all around him. It seemed that the Russian authorities had arrived in force. Sarov's men were heavily out-numbered but were still fighting back. They knew they had nothing to lose.

The magnet reached the submarine. Alex dropped it towards the silver chest, remembering how delicately it had been done by

Conrad. He was less skilled – and winced as the heavy disc smashed into the top. Damn! He would set the thing off himself if he wasn't careful. He pressed the button in the control stick a second time and actually felt the magnet come alive and knew that the nuclear bomb was in its grip. He pulled back, lifting the magnetic hoist. The silver chest came clear of the submarine.

Now, a centimetre at a time, he swung the arm of the crane over the water, bringing the nuclear bomb back towards the harbour. A second bullet slammed into the crane and the window shattered right next to his head. Alex cried out. Glass fragments showered over him. He thought he was going to be blinded. But when he next looked up, the nuclear bomb was over the quay and he knew that he was nearly finished.

He lowered it. At the very moment it touched the ground, there was another explosion, louder and closer than any that had gone before. But it wasn't nuclear. One of the warehouses had shattered. Another was on fire. A second helicopter had arrived and it was strafing the ground, whipping dust and debris into the air. It was hard to be sure, but Alex thought that Sarov's men were losing ground. There seemed to be less return fire. Well, in a few more seconds, it wouldn't matter.

All he had to do was retrieve the plastic card.

He pulled the magnet clear, jumped from the crane, then ran over to the chest. He could see the card, half protruding from the slot where Sarov had inserted it. The lights were still blinking, the numbers spinning. There was less gunfire around him now. Looking over his shoulder, he saw more men in blue edging slowly into the compound, coming in from all sides. He reached down and pulled out the card. The lights on the nuclear bomb went out. The numbers disappeared. He had done it!

"Put it back."

The words were softly spoken but each one dripped menace. Alex looked up and saw Sarov in front of him. Somehow he must have learned that the compound was under attack and had made his way back. How much time had passed since the two of them had last faced each other? Thirty minutes? An hour? However long it had been, Sarov had changed. He was smaller, shrunken. The light in his eyes had gone out and what little colour there had been in his skin seemed to have become muddied. He had been wounded fighting his way back into the harbour. There was a rip in his jacket and a slowly spreading red stain. His left hand hung useless.

But his right hand was holding a gun.

"It's over, General," Alex said. "Conrad is dead.

The Russian army is here. Someone must have tipped them off."

Sarov shook his head. "I can still detonate the bomb. There is an override. You and I will die. But the end result will be the same."

"A better world?"

"That's all I ever wanted, Alex. All of this...! I was only ever doing what I believed in."

Alex felt an enormous tiredness creeping up on him. He weighed the card in his hand. It was strange really. From one Skeleton Key to another. It all came down to this.

Sarov raised the gun. The blood was spreading more rapidly now. He swayed on his feet. "Give me the card or I will shoot you," he said.

Alex lifted the card then suddenly flicked it. It spun twice in the air, then disappeared into the water. "Go ahead then, if that's what you want," he said. "Shoot me!"

Sarov's eyes flickered over to the lost card, then back to Alex. "Why...?" he whispered.

"I'd rather be dead than have a father like you," Alex said.

There were voices shouting. Footsteps coming nearer.

"Goodbye, Alex," Sarov said.

He raised the gun and fired a single shot.

AFTER ALEX

"We've lost Alex Rider," Mrs Jones said. "I'm sorry, Alan. I know it's not what you wanted to hear. But that's the end of it."

The head of MI6 Special Operations and his number two were having lunch together in a restaurant near Liverpool Street Station. They ate there frequently, although not often together. The restaurant was in a basement with low, vaulted ceilings, soft lighting and bare brick walls. Blunt liked the starched white tablecloths and the old-fashioned service. Also, the food was poor so few people came there. That was useful when he wanted to have a conversation such as this.

"Alex did very well," he muttered.

"Oh yes. I had an email from Joe Byrne in

Virginia. Of course, he was upset about the loss of his own two agents in the underwater cave, but he was full of praise for Alex. He definitely owes us a favour ... which will at least be useful in the future." She took a bread roll and broke it in half. "It wouldn't surprise me if the CIA didn't start training their own teenage spy now. The Americans are always copying our ideas."

"When we're not copying theirs," Blunt remarked.

"That's true."

They paused as the waiter came over with the first course. Grilled sardines for Mrs Jones, soup for Blunt. Neither dish looked particularly appetizing but that didn't matter. Neither of them had much of an appetite.

"I've looked through the files and I think I have the general picture," Blunt said. "But perhaps you can fill me in on some of the details. In particular, I'd like to know how the Russian authorities found out about Sarov in time."

"That was because of what happened at Edinburgh Airport," Mrs Jones explained. She looked down at her plate. There were four sardines lying side by side, complete with heads and tails. If it was possible for a fish to look unhappy, these had managed it. She squeezed lemon over them. The juice formed tears beneath the unblinking eyes.

"Alex ran into a security guard called George Prescott," she went on. "He'd managed to escape from Sarov's plane using a gadget Smithers had given him."

"I don't recall authorizing Smithers—" Blunt began.

"Alex wanted to use a telephone," Mrs Jones cut in. "Obviously, he was going to warn us about Murmansk, what Sarov was planning. This man, Prescott, stopped him."

"Unfortunate."

"Yes. It must have been very frustrating. Alex actually told him that he was a spy and that he was working for us, but then Sarov caught up with him. Prescott was killed – and that was the end of it. Or it would have been ... but we were extremely fortunate. Prescott had a radio transmitter clipped to his jacket. It was turned on throughout his conversation with Alex and his office heard every word that was said. Of course, they didn't believe Alex either, but when Prescott was found with a bullet in his head they put two and two together and got on to us as fast as they could. I was the one who alerted the authorities at Murmansk and I must say that the Russians acted very promptly. They pulled a naval force together, plus two helicopter gunships, and stormed the yard."

"What happened to the bomb?"

"They have it. According to their people, it would have been big enough to blow a sizeable hole in the Kola Peninsular. The fallout would have contaminated Norway, Finland and, for that matter, most of Great Britain. And I really do think the backlash would have been enough to force Kiriyenko out of power. Nobody likes him very much anyway."

"Where is Kiriyenko?" Blunt's soup was almost cold. He had forgotten what was meant to be in it.

"The Cuban authorities found him locked up on Skeleton Key. Shouting his head off and blaming everyone except himself." Mrs Jones shook her head. "He's back in Moscow now. Sarov gave him a bad scare, but then he gave us all a bad scare. If it hadn't been for Alex, who knows what might have happened."

"What do the Cubans have to say about all this?"

"They've disowned Sarov. Nothing to do with them. They had no idea what he was planning. What's so terrifying is that he nearly got away with it!"

"If it hadn't been for Alex Rider..."

The two of them finished their first course in silence.

"Where is Alex now?" Blunt asked eventually.

"He's home."

"How is he?"

Mrs Jones sighed. "It would seem that Sarov shot himself," she said. "Alex was standing right in front of him. The trouble with you, Alan, is that you've never had children and you refuse to accept the fact that, at the end of the day, Alex is only a child. He's already been through far more than any fourteen year old could possibly be expected to ... and this last mission! I would say it was his toughest yet. And at the very end he actually saw what Sarov did!"

"I suppose Sarov didn't want to be taken alive," Blunt muttered.

"I wish it was as simple as that. It seems that Sarov had some sort of ... attachment to Alex. He saw him as the son he had lost. Alex rejected him and it pushed him over the edge. *That's* why he did it. He couldn't live with himself any more."

Blunt signalled and a waiter came over and poured the wine. It was unusual for the two spy-masters to drink at lunchtime but Blunt had selected a half bottle of Chablis, which had been sitting in an ice bucket beside their table. Another waiter served the main courses. The food sat on the table untouched.

"What happened with that business with the triads?" Blunt asked.

"Oh – I've sorted all that out. We had a couple of their people in jail and I arranged for them to be released. Flown back to Hong Kong. It was enough. They'll leave Alex alone."

"So why do you say we've lost him?"

"The truth is, we shouldn't have used him in the first place."

"We didn't use him. It was the CIA."

"You know that doesn't make any difference." Mrs Jones tasted the wine. "The point is, I was the one who debriefed him and all I can say is … he's not the same. I know, I've said this all before. But I was seriously worried about him, Alan. He was so silent and withdrawn. He'd been badly hurt."

"Any broken bones?"

"For heaven's sake! Children can be hurt in other ways! I'm sorry, but I do feel very strongly about this. We can't use him again. It isn't fair."

"Life isn't fair." Blunt picked up his own glass. "I think you're forgetting that Alex has just saved the world. That boy is fast becoming one of our most effective operatives. He's the best secret weapon we have. We can't afford to be sentimental about him. We'll let him rest. I dare say he needs to catch up at school, and then there's the summer holidays. But you know as well as I do, if the need arises, there's nothing to discuss. We'll use him again. And again..."

Mrs Jones put down her knife and fork. "I'm suddenly not very hungry," she said.

Blunt glanced at her. "I hope you're not getting a conscience," he said. "If you're really worried about Alex, bring him in and we'll have a little heart to heart."

Mrs Jones looked her boss straight in the eye. "He may have trouble finding yours," she said.

The next day was a Saturday. Alex got up late, showered, dressed and went down to a breakfast that his housekeeper, Jack Starbright, had prepared for him. She had cooked all his favourite things but he ate little of it, sitting at the table in silence. Jack was desperately worried about him. The day before she had tried to get him to see a doctor and for the first time in his life he had snapped at her. Now she wasn't sure what to do. If things didn't get better she would talk to that woman – Mrs Jones. Jack wasn't supposed to know what was going on, but she had a good idea. She would make them do something. Things couldn't go on like this.

"What you going to do today?" she asked.

Alex shrugged. There was a bandage round his hand where the metal pole had cut him and a number of grazes on his face. Worst of all though were the bruises around his neck. Conrad had certainly left his mark.

"D'you want to see a film?"

"No. I thought I'd go for a walk."

"I'll come with you, if you like."

"No. Thanks, Jack, but I'm OK on my own."

Ten minutes later, Alex left the house. The weather forecast had said it would be a bright day but in fact it was close and cloudy. He started walking towards the King's Road, wanting to lose himself in the crowds. He had no real idea where he was going. He just needed to think.

Sarov was dead. Alex had turned away as the man had raised the gun towards his own heart, not bearing to see any more. Minutes later it had all been over. The Repair Yard had been secured, the bomb removed. Alex himself had been whisked away by helicopter, first to a hospital in Moscow and then back to London. Someone had told him that Kiriyenko wanted to see him. There was talk of a medal. Alex had declined. He just wanted to go home.

And that's where he was. Everything had worked out all right. He was a hero!

So why did he feel like this? And how exactly *was* it that he felt? Depressed? Exhausted? He was both of those things – but worse still, he felt empty. It was almost as if he had died in the Submarine Repair Shipyard of Murmansk and had somehow returned to London as a ghost. Life was all around him but he wasn't a part of it. Even lying in his own bed, in his own house, he felt he no longer belonged.

So much had happened to him but he wasn't allowed to talk about it with anyone. He couldn't even tell Jack. She would be horrified and upset – and there was nothing she could do anyway. He had missed more weeks of school and knew that it wasn't just the work he would have to catch up with. Friendships move on too. People already thought he was weird. It wouldn't be long before nobody was talking to him at all.

He would never have a father. He knew this now. He would never have an ordinary life. Somehow, he had got himself trapped. A ghost. That was what he had become.

Alex hadn't heard the car stop behind him.

He hadn't heard the door open and close. But there were suddenly footsteps running up behind him and before he could move, a hand had been thrown around his chest.

"Alex!"

He spun round. "Sabina!"

Sabina Pleasure was standing in front of him, panting after the short run, wearing a Robbie Williams T-shirt and jeans, a brightly coloured straw bag over her shoulder. Her face was lit up with pleasure. "Thank goodness I found you. I've been after you for weeks. You never gave me your phone number but it's lucky I knew your address. Mum and Dad drove me over..." She gestured at her parents, sitting in the car. They both raised a hand, waving at Alex through the windscreen. "I was going to look in just in case you were at home. And here you are!" She looked at his neck, examining his bruises. "You look terrible! Have you been involved in a car smash?"

"Not exactly."

"Anyway, Alex," she interrupted. "I'm really pissed off with you. I saved your life in Cornwall, in case you don't remember – although I have to say that giving you the kiss of life on the beach *was* the high point of the holiday – and the next thing I knew, you'd simply vanished. I didn't even get so much as a thank-you card."

"Well, I was, sort of ... busy."

"Being James Bond, I suppose?"

"Well..." Alex didn't know what to say.

Sabina took his arm. "You can tell me all about it later. Mum and Dad have invited you to lunch and we want to talk about the South of France."

"What about it?"

"That's where we're going this summer. And you're coming too. We've got some friends who've lent us a house and a pool and it's going to be great." She looked closely at his face. "Don't tell me you had other plans?"

Alex smiled. "No, Sabina, I haven't got any plans."

"That's settled then. Now, what do you want for lunch? I fancy an Italian – but he's been ignoring me so you'll have to do!" She laughed.

Alex and Sabina walked down the street together. Alex glanced up. The clouds had parted and the sun was out.

It looked as if it was going to be a bright day after all.

STORMBREAKER
Anthony Horowitz

Meet Alex Rider, the reluctant teenage spy.

When his guardian dies in suspicious circum-stances, fourteen-year-old Alex Rider finds his world turned upside down.

Within days he's gone from schoolboy to super-spy. Forcibly recruited into MI6, Alex has to take part in gruelling SAS training exercises. Then, armed with his own special set of secret gadgets, he's off on his first mission.

His destination is the depths of Cornwall, where Middle-Eastern multimillionaire Herod Sayle is producing his state-of-the-art Stormbreaker computers. Sayle's offered to give one free to every school in the country – but MI6 think there's more to the gift than meets the eye.

Only Alex can find out the truth. But time is run-ning out and Alex soon finds himself in mortal danger. It looks as if his first assignment may well be his last...

Explosive, thrilling, action-packed, *Stormbreaker* reveals Anthony Horowitz at his brilliant best.

"Suspenseful and exciting." *Books for Keeps*

"The perfect hero ... genuine 21st century stuff." *The Daily Telegraph*

POINT BLANC
Anthony Horowitz

Alex Rider, teenage superspy, is back!

Fourteen-year-old Alex Rider, reluctant MI6 spy, is back at school trying to adapt to his new double life ... and to double homework.

But MI6 have other plans for him.

Investigations into the "accidental" deaths of two of the world's most powerful men have revealed just one link. Both had a son attending Point Blanc Academy – an exclusive school for rebellious rich kids, run by the sinister Dr Grief and set high on an isolated mountain peak in the French Alps.

Armed only with a false ID and a new collection of brilliantly disguised gadgets, Alex must infiltrate the academy as a pupil and establish the truth about what is really happening there. Can he alert the world to what he discovers before it is too late?

"Horowitz will grip you with suspense, daring and cheek – and that's just the first page! Prepare for action scenes as fast as a movie. A stormin' follow-up to *Stormbreaker*."
The Times

THE FALCON'S MALTESER
Anthony Horowitz

"Johnny Naples opened his mouth and tried to speak. 'The falcon...' he said. Then a nasty, bubbling sound."

When vertically challenged Johnny Naples entrusts Tim Diamond with a package worth over three million pounds, he's making a big mistake. For Tim Diamond is probably the worst detective in the entire world. Next day, Johnny's dead. Tim gets the blame, his smart, wisecracking younger brother Nick gets the package – and every crook in town is out to get them!

"Any child with a quick sense of humour should love it... An abundance of jokes, most of them first-class." *The Times Literary Supplement*

PUBLIC ENEMY NUMBER TWO
Anthony Horowitz

"So there I was in a maximum-security prison outside London, accused of theft, trespass, criminal damage and cruelty to animals... Me ... public enemy number two!"

Framed for a jewel robbery, quick-thinking young Nick Diamond finds himself sharing a prison cell with Johnny Powers, Public Enemy Number One. His only chance of rescuing the situation is to nail the Fence, the country's master criminal. First, though, Nick has to get out of jail – which is where his older brother Tim, the world's worst private detective, comes in... But with Ma Powers and her gang waiting to greet the jailbirds, the heat is really on for the Diamond brothers in this explosive adventure!

"Horowitz has become a writer who converts boys to reading." *The Times*

SOUTH BY SOUTH EAST
Anthony Horowitz

"McGuffin had finished talking. The telephone was dead and any minute now he'd be joining it. The stuff he had spilled down the coat was blood, his own blood..."

Tim Diamond, the world's worst private detective is broke – as his much smarter younger brother Nick is quick to remind him. So, when a mysterious stranger offers Tim a wad of money for his overcoat, it seems like a stroke of good luck. But there are worse things in life than being broke. Being pumped full of lead for one – which is what happens to the stranger and could soon be the fate of the Diamond brothers too, unless they can outwit the unknown assassin on their tail!

"A first-class children's novelist."
The Times Educational Supplement